38

WRITTEN BY: JOHN S. BECKMANN

PrairieUprising.com

HERE
WERE HANGED
38
SIOUX INDIANS
DEC. 26TH 1862

ILLUSTRATED BY: JOHN F. BECKMANN

stampedePress.com

Publisher and Design
JOHN F. BECKMANN

Editor
JOHN S. BECKMANN

stampedePress.com

Published by
Stampede Press
214 NE 11th Ave
Faribault, Minnesota 55021

www.stampedepress.com

ISBN-13: 978-0615615479

Designed by John F. Beckmann

1st edition August 2012

38

To the memory of my father, John D. Beckmann, whose interest in the Great Sioux Uprising inspired this work.

Introduction

On the
Hanging Stone

History is what we have agreed to remember. But memories differ and
fade. For various reasons, the Great Sioux Uprising of 1862 was almost forgotten. The war occurred around the time that the battle of Antietam dyed red the
meadows and streams of western Maryland. An obscurely motivated, ugly little
bout of ethnic cleansing in a remote northwestern territory had little claim on the
national attention. And when the catastrophe was concluded, the memories that it
engendered were nasty, inconclusive, and difficult to assimilate to any prevailing
narrative about the scope and course of American history. Some things are best
forgotten.

Nothing is clear about this conflict. Even it's name is contested. Were
the murderous events in the summer of 1862 a "conflict," a "war," an "insurrec-
tion" or "uprising" or some uncategorized type of terroristic race riot? On the
hundredth anniversary of the war, in 1962, the catastrophe was called "The Great
Sioux Uprising". Under that title, books were published and a Minneapolis
newspaper issued a comic strip retelling the story in three-color panels that
looked like the Sunday funny-pages. A couple decades later, someone noticed
that the word "Sioux" was an appellation used by enemies of that tribe – the
Chippewa employed the designation as a derogatory term and it may have meant
something like "snakes" or "ancestral enemy." So the massacres and reprisals of
1862 were collectively renamed the ""The Dakota War". "War" wasn't exactly
fitting to describe a course of vicious ethnic cleansing and, so, historians settled
on the phrase the "Lakota Conflict." "Lakota" is an affectation like the vigor-
ously rolled "r's" and gulped "n" and "l" sounds newscasters currently use when
pronouncing place-names in Honduras and Mexico. "Lakota" simulates the way
that the name of the tribe, or the western faction of the tribe, would be spoken by
one of it's members. Like the self-designations for most Indian tribes, the word
is laudatory – it apparently means something like "friends" or "allies."

"Lakota Conflict" springs trippingly from the tongue. The phrase sounds
like something a lawyer might plead or a policy wonk debate. In fact, the

"conflict" was several months of mutually sustained murder culminating the largest mass execution ever perpetrated by sanctioned legal authority in American history – the death by hanging of 38 Lakota men in Mankato on December 1862.

Briefly summarized, here is what happened: the Dakota Indians were a group of Siouan speaking tribes roughly divided into seven ancestral groups or "council fires." At first contact with European explorers, the Dakotas seemed to occupy territory near the Great Lakes, although some authorities place them in modern day Tennessee and Kentucky. No less than the white invaders, American Indian tribes were rapacious for territorial acquisition and fought for land enthusiastically, conquering and being conquered since time immemorial. Ousted from their hunting range in the woodlands by the firearms of European invaders, the Dakota learned to use rifles and gunpowder themselves and transformed themselves, ultimately, into the famous light cavalry that destroyed Custer and Fetterman on the high planes a generation after the debacle in Minnesota. The tribal group involved in the Minnesota massacre were Santee Sioux, that is, the eastern-most clan, essentially woodland Indians commencing their transition to plains nomads – their soldier societies were hardened by two-hundred years continuous warfare with Assiniboine (Chippewa) Indians that lived in the forests around the headwaters of the Mississippi.

The Santee Dakota occupying the southern half of present-day Minnesota found themselves besieged by hordes of European settlers, most of them German immigrants fleeing political unrest in Deutsch-speaking central Europe. The land was big and sparsely settled and initially the pioneers and the Dakotas lived together peacefully. Pressure for land, however, induced a contractual settlement between the Dakota and the encroaching settlers (together with Federal territorial authorities.) In 1851, and later 1858, the Santee agreed to sell vast tracts of territory to the United States government in exchange for reservation lands guaranteed to their people in the verdant river valley of the upper Minnesota, between Mankato, Minnesota and the Big Stone Lake on what is now the South Dakota border. In addition, the government was to pay annuities as compensation for the land purchased by treaty, the 1851 agreement at Traverse des Sioux. On the strength of this agreement, the Santee Dakota moved into villages along the Minnesota River clustered around two Indian Agencies, the Lower Sioux Agency near modern Morton, Minnesota and the Yellow Medicine Agency, near missionary stations close to present-day Montevideo. Dissident members of the Santee bands didn't accept the agreement – treaties with Indian tribes were perennially afflicted by problems of political authority: to the present-day, it is never entirely clear who has the authority to bind a tribal group to legal agreements. But the majority of the Santee Dakota seemed willing to cut their hair, learn farming skills, and settle down near the river, reserving to themselves a right to periodic bison-hunting forays on the western plains as a way of preserving their cultural perquisites. The war-chief of the Santee Dakota, Little Crow, (Thaoyate Dute) traveled to Washington, glad-handed politicians and joined the Episcopal Church.

Trouble quickly developed. Renegade tribal members massacred a group of settlers at Spirit Lake, Iowa, leading to an inconclusive campaign against the outlaw part of the tribe. The campaign failed and the malefactors went unpunished. Then, crops failed and government annuities promised for mid-summer 1862 were delayed. The Dakota were deeply in debt to Agency merchants who refused credit to the starving Indians. The government default on annuity payments, probably caused by Civil War funding pressure, enraged the Santee. Allegedly, a trader at the Lower Agency, one Andrew Myrick, when importuned to distribute flour and other foodstuffs held in his warehouses, said that "if the Sioux are hungry, they can eat grass."

On August 17, 1862, a hunting party approached a farm site near Hutchinson, Minnesota and, after some kind of altercation – legend has it that the quarrel originated in the theft of some eggs – murdered several families of settlers. The killers fled to villages along the Minnesota River and announced that war had begun with the hated white settlers. On the Sunday morning before the massacre began, Little Crow had attended worship services at the Episcopal church near his comfortable frame house. Witnesses recalled him shaking hands with the preacher and the white parishioners. Communities of white settlers and Indian clans were small, interacted daily, and often were intermarried – everyone knew everyone else. When the young men, fearful of government retribution, rode their stinking, sweat-drenched horses into the villages near the Lower Agency, no one knew what exactly to do. At a tempestuous tribal council meeting, Little Crow reluctantly announced that he would lead a war against the white pioneers. The war chief expressed grave doubts about the success of the endeavor – but, he seems to have thought that the Civil War, which had drained the territory of soldiers and fighting men, might be a sufficient diversion to allow some faint hope that sudden attacks on settlements scattered across the prairie might expel the white pioneers.

The next morning, Sioux war parties killed the traders and their families at the Lower Agency, murdering the callous Nathan Myrick and stuffing the mouth of his corpse with grass. The Santee, then, engaged in a course of savage ethnic cleansing. White families were slaughtered in their cabins and on the roads as they attempted to flee. Women were raped and mutilated; children were butchered. This was ethnic cleansing similar to 20th century catastrophes in Rwanda and Serbia – in this kind of massacre, you knew the first name of the men who came to kill you. Your in-laws participated in your butchery. As you were cut down, you could call out, not only the names of your murderers, but also the names of their wives and children. People died horribly in a state of bemusement – why are people that I have considered my friends and trading partners coming to hack me into pieces?

After a few days of carnage, the small villages on the prairie had been destroyed, the settlers were mostly dead, and hundreds of women and children had been taken prisoner. Little Crow understood that success required that his soldiers capture Fort Ridgely, a weakly defended outpost supervising the reservation, and New Ulm, a fairly large German settlement down river from the Lower Agency. The troops at Fort Ridgely had howitzers and, during two rather desultory attacks, repelled the Indian war parties. The Dakota regrouped and mounted a major assault on New Ulm. This was a battle unlike any other fight conducted on American soil, a sort of mini-Stalingrad in which combatants fought house to house, shooting one another from the cellars of burning ruins and sniping from windmills also set afire. The defenders of the town, which was clogged with thousands of terrified refugees, burned it down to create fields of fire and, after hours of desperate fighting from behind barricades of household furniture and beer kegs, drove back the Santee war parties, which numbered over 600 men.

After the Santee Sioux failed to capture New Ulm, the war was lost. Federal troops engaged the Indians and defeated them in several small fights. A burial party was ambushed at Birch Coulee with sizeable loss of life, but, ultimately, it was only a matter of time before the superior military force of the United States army scattered the Indians and commenced operations to "drive them forever" from the boundaries of the State. The Santee Sioux having failed in their effort to ethnically cleanse southern Minnesota of white invaders now found themselves on the receiving end of similar reprisals. Little Crow fled to Canada with some of the most bellicose of the Santee, but the remainder of the tribe surrendered and was promptly interred in a concentration camp on the river flats near Fort Snelling, near St. Paul. Military tribunals were quickly convened to try warriors accused of rape and murder. After short hearings, many of them lasting less than five minutes, 303 Santee men were condemned to death. Local clergy intervened and petitions for clemency were made to President Lincoln. With characteristic compassion and alacrity, Lincoln reviewed the trial transcripts and decreed that only 39 warriors, those accused of the most vicious crimes, be executed.

On December 26, 1862, thirty-eight Dakota men were hanged at Mankato (one of the condemned had been pardoned at the last moment). Little Crow was murdered in the summer of 1863 while raiding for horses near Hutchinson, Minnesota. His head was cut-off and his body tossed in an offal pit. Little Crow's scalp was taken to St. Paul where it was displayed for many years in the marble corridors of the State Historical Society. (The relic was buried in a family plot near Flandrau, South Dakota in the presence of Little Crow's surviving relatives about twenty years ago). Little Crow's son, Wowinapa (also known as Thomas Wakeman) founded the YMCA among the Dakota Sioux.

When I was a small boy, my family visited the home where Dr. William Worrel Mayo had lived and practiced medicine in LeSeuer, Minnesota. In those days, LeSeuer was a sleepy town stretched along a low, water-logged shelf of land a few yards above a bend in the Minnesota River. The town was green, streets arched with old trees, and, in my memory, a stifling, humid, tropical heat always lingers over the small houses and quiet lanes in the valley. Green Giant had a pea-pack at the town's outskirts and, on a billboard atop the bluff overlooking the village, there was a robust, grinning green colossus.

Dr. Mayo was the father of two sons, William and Charles, who founded the famous Mayo Clinic, eighty miles to the east in Rochester. The historic home was small, like a cottage in the British countryside and I remember it having a vaguely Tudor appearance. The inside was dark and smelled of old upholstery and mildew. In Dr. Mayo's study, there was a skeleton sulking in a corner. The bones were articulated and hung like a coat on a mahogany coat-rack. The tour guide, an elderly lady, told us that bones were the mortal remains of a notorious Sioux war-chief, Cut Nose. My father had studied the Sioux Uprising in depth and we had many books on that subject at home. Cut-Nose was a very bad Indian, the kind of man who butchered children in front of their mothers, before superintending the dismemberment of the screaming women. Convicted by a military tribunal in November 1862, he was one of the 38 Dakota men hanged at Mankato. The old lady told us that, in the dead of night, Dr. Mayo took a cart down to the river flats at Mankato where the corpses of the dead Sioux had been interred in shallow, muddy graves. With a couple of assistants, he extracted Cut-Nose's body from the earth and hauled it back to LeSeuer. Medical specimens were rare and hard-to-come-by on the Minnesota frontier. The old woman said that Dr. Mayo had dissected the corpse to teach his two sons anatomy. I pictured the body sprawled on the living room table, amid the florid Victorian furniture, the wreaths of hair displayed under domes of glass, the antimacassars and ottomans. I imagined two little boys, something like my brother and I, groping in the dead Indian's bowels. She pointed to the bones in the gloomy corner of the study. The skeleton was brown and looked moist, glistening slightly the way a fetus pickled in formaldehyde reflects a faintly yellow, lunar glint. The skeleton was a cage of bones surmounted by a bemused-looking hollow skull. "And this is Cut Nose himself," the old lady said.

Like most stories about the Sioux Uprising, the tale was probably false, at least with respect to identifying the skeleton as Cut Nose's remains. The two Mayo boys weren't born until after 1863 and so, it seems, doubtful that they participated in the actual anatomical dissection of the Indian warrior. It does seem clear that Dr. Mayo dissected the body of the notorious war chief, but, apparently, with several other local physicians. Furthermore, in 2000, when Cut Nose's body parts were finally repatriated to his surviving relatives and buried somewhere near the tribal casino at Jackpot Junction (Morton, Minnesota), only a couple fragments remained. His skull had been found, reportedly, in some doctor's office within the Mayo Clinic in Rochester, kept as a paper-weight, and a typing-sheet sized strip of tanned human flesh, tattooed with his name, was sent back to Minnesota from a small municipal museum in Grand Rapids, Michigan. The skeleton that I saw in Le Seuer was, indeed, probably Indian – but collected from the slums of Calcutta or Bombay.

I am writing these words as a preface to my book *38*. That book is a work of the imagination and so, unlike history, has the advantage of being true, or as nearly true as I could make it. Facts presumed to be accurate and presented as the historical record are always untrue. Paradoxically, this is because they are merely facts – a fact is always incomplete in itself and subject to the vagaries of recollection and opinion. This is particularly true of facts that are colored by horror, fear, and rage – ordinarily the emotions attendant upon the lurid events that people remember as "historical."

Two examples drawn from histories of the Sioux Uprising are exemplary. First, consider the case of Andrew Myrick's callous remark that "if the Sioux are hungry, they can eat grass" (In some less refined versions: "grass or their own dung.") This statement is reasonably well attested. We know its alleged date, August 15, 1862 and the names of witnesses to the remark are, also, cited. Little Crow, with a group of tribal leaders, went to the warehouses at the Lower Sioux Agency, said that his people were starving, and demanded that flour and other provisions be distributed. Little Crow remarked that "when people are starving they take matters into their own hands." Myrick responded with the infamous insult, an incident universally recorded in all accounts of the conflict. A government translator present is said to have refused to put Myrick's words into Lakota as unduly inflammatory. One of the Sioux warriors asked a missionary who was present to translate the statement and the clergyman is reported to have obliged instantly in a loud and clear voice. Big Eagle, a very reliable source among of the Sioux, recalled the incident vividly. Reverend Stephen Riggs reports the episode in his memoir *Mary and I, Forty years among the Sioux* published in 1880.

But there is something more than a little bit suspicious about this famous historical anecdote. First, the Sioux said to have heard this deadly insult didn't take any action at that time. The first organized attack on white settlers was on Monday, the 19th of August, only after the hunting party had killed several families in Acton Township in the dispute over the eggs. Accordingly, Myrick's infamous remark didn't trigger any immediate response, something that seems unlikely given the inflammatory nature of the statement. Second, the statement has a literary precedent that suggests that the entire incident is apocryphal. Charles Dickens' *Tale of Two Cities* was an enormous international bestseller published as a serial in *All the Year Round* and, then, in first edition, in 1859. Dickens was the most renowned novelist in the world and his works were universally distributed and read. Highly educated missionaries on the Minnesota frontier were well read and, undoubtedly, knew Dickens' novels well. Perhaps, Myrick was a Dickens' fan also – we don't know the merchant's reading habits.

In *The Tale of Two Cities*, Dickens mentions at several points a French minister, Joseph-Francois Foulon, a Counselor of State of the *ancien regime*, said to have told the starving peasants "to eat grass." Mimicking Carlyles's ejaculatory style, Dickens writes:

Villain Foulon taken, my sister! Old Foulon taken, my mother!
Miscreant Foulon taken, my daughter! Then, a score of others ran into
the midst of these, beating their breasts, tearing their hair and screaming,
Foulon alive! Foulon who told the starving people that they might eat
grass! Foulon, who told my old father that he might eat grass, when I
had to bread to give him! Foulon, who told my baby it might suck grass,
when these breasts were dry with want!

Later, in this same frenzied peroration, Dickens imagines the French mob crying: *Rend Foulon in pieces and dig him into the ground, that the grass may grow from him.* (See *The sea still rises*, Chapter 22 of *The Tale of Two Cities*).

Dickens recounted the story of Foulon's callous remark about a year and a half before the events at the Lower Sioux Agency involving Myrick and Little Crow in August 1862. It certainly seems highly suspicious that Myrick uses the exact phrase attributed to the much-maligned Foulon by Dickens, and other writers on the French Revolution. Several surmises are warranted. Perhaps, the story is completely apocryphal and simply a parable about callous pride derived entirely from the lore of the French revolution and Dickens' novel. (Whether Big Eagle had read Dickens or knew about his novel is unclear – I'm certainly not willing to exclude the possibility that English-reading Sioux Indians might not have read and enjoyed the works of Dickens like everyone else in the Victorian world.) Possibly, Myrick made some kind of nasty comment and it was later confused with something that the informant had read in Dickens' famous book. Or, I suppose, it is possible that Myrick knew the book and was ironically citing it when he uttered those words. My point, however, is that one of the most famous anecdotes explaining the cause of the Sioux Uprising is, most probably, fictional or, at least, derived and exemplified by a parallel incident in a widely distributed novel.

Even more salient questions arise in the context of Little Crow's famous speech, allegedly delivered in a war council on the eve of the attack on the Lower Agency. The young men who had committed murders at Acton appeared among the villages near the Lower Sioux Agency and a delegation of tribal leaders hurried to Little Crow's fine, wood and plaster house to seek his counsel. Big Eagle was present and he recalls Little Crow "sitting up in bed" to hear the bad news.

Little Crow is supposed to have counseled against the war and said that it would surely be lost. Someone attributed his reluctance to engage in fighting to cowardice. This remark inflamed the war chief and he, then, delivered a famous oration:

Braves, you are like little children, you know not what you are doing.
You are full of the white-man's devil water. You are like dogs in the Hot
Moon when they run mad and snap at their own shadows.

We are only little herds of buffaloes left scattered; the great herds that once covered the prairies are no more. See! The white men are like the locusts when they fly so thick that the whole sky is a snowstorm.

You may kill one, two, ten; yes, as many as the leaves on the forest yonder – and their brothers will not miss them. Kill one, two, ten, and ten times ten will come to kill you. Count your fingers all day long, and white men with guns in their hands will come faster than you can count.

Braves, you are little children, you are fools. You will die like jackrabbits when the hungry wolves hunt them in the Hungry Moon.

Taoyateduta (Little Crow) is no coward, he will die with you.

Now, undoubtably, this is thrilling stuff. The speech has a quasi-Shake-spearian flavor and, yet, reminds us exactly how dignified Indian chiefs were supposed to sound. In fact, the speech has the feeling of something that you might hear in a Hollywood movie. Every historian who has recently written on the Sioux Uprising reports this speech or one of its variants. For instance, a Texas professor, Gary Clayton Anderson, the author of a highly regarded 1986 bi-ography of the war chief, *Little Crow, Spokesman for the Sioux*, quotes a version of this speech in its entirety and does not suggest any reservations about the au-thenticity of the oration. Anderson's book bears the imprint of the Minnesota Historical Society publishing house. No one seems to suspect that the speech is simply too good to be true.

But there are many reasons to doubt the authenticity of the speech. First, internal evidence suggests that something is amiss. In 1862, the buffalo herds had not been eradicated. The destruction of those herds occurred during the western expansion after the Civil War – therefore, either Little Crow is prophetic in his remark about the vanished bison, or someone has misremembered the ora-tion in the context of later events. During the last quarter of the 19th century, the notion that the "red man" was "vanishing" with the buffalo that he hunted was a sentimental truism. But that idea didn't exist in the summer of 1862. (Similarly, would Little Crow really have quoted Jesus Christ – "you know not what you are doing" – to a group of inflamed war chiefs?)

Big Eagle said that he was in the room when the council with Little Crow oc-curred. He doesn't report anything like this oration. Instead, he recalled that Little Crow, apparently upset about being awakened, made a bitter remark about the outcome of a recent tribal election, saying words to the effect: "You elected Traveling Hail (to be your leader). Go talk to him." Further, Big Eagle, rather prosaically recalled that Little Crow concluded the war council by saying: "Let us kill the traders and divide their goods." William Watts Folwell, probably the most conscientious historian of the great uprising, doesn't mention the speech in his magisterial study published in 1924 and relying heavily on the first-hand rec-ollections of participants on both sides of the war. The speech seems to enter history via Thomas Hughes self-published *Indian Chiefs of Southern Minnesota*, printed in St. Cloud in 1927. Hughes claims that he "had the speech from Little Crow's son" and set it down to show the power of the great man's oratory – Hughes says that he has "copied" the speech. But from what source? Did Wowinape, Little Crow's fourteen-year-old son, write the speech down and carry it around with him as a document of some sort? This seems unlikely.

In fact, the speech is first printed in a book of verse published in Chicago in 1891, the year that concluded with the massacre at Wounded Knee. This peculiar volume is entitled The Feast of the Virgins and other poems and was written by a Minneapolis lawyer, Hanford L. Gordon. Gordon reproduces the speech, claiming that he "made a copy" from Wowinape (Thomas Eastman) who "had an excellent recollection" of the event that had occurred 29 years earlier. (Wowinape died in 1880 and so Gordon's recollections of Wowinape's memories were a decade old when he committed the speech to print in 1891). Gordon prints the speech in an extended footnote to the title verse, Feast of the Virgins, a pastiche of Indian themes heavily influenced by Henry Longfellow's *Hiawatha*. Simply stated, the sources for Little Crow's speech, a oration that has entered the cultural mythology surrounding the Great Sioux Uprising, are exceedingly suspect. Like Chief Seattle's famous, and apocryphal, admonitory speech – it seems that Little Crow's oration was largely invented by white admirers.

As is the case with *38*, it seems that Little Crow's famous oration is a work of the imagination. But, as was said in another context, when the legend becomes the fact, print the legend.

Nothing much remains from the Great Sioux Uprising. When I was a child, German was still spoken on the streets of New Ulm and there was a shabby restaurant downtown that boasted some bullet holes pecked in its old walls during the famous siege. No one speaks German in New Ulm any more and I'm not entirely certain that the language is even offered for study at the local High School. The building defaced by bullets was torn down many years ago. In south central Minnesota today, you are far more likely to encounter someone speaking Spanish than any tongue originating in *Mitteleuropa*. At Traverse des Sioux, there is an old cemetery and you can see some graves inscribed with names, half illegible, above the weather-beaten legend: *Killed by the Sioux*. The cemetery is large and contains many luminaries of the pioneer era, but, last time I was at that place, it was overgrown with weeds – the prairie was reclaiming the graveyard. Other rural cemeteries on gravel roads in the country contain similar headstones. These old graveyards are forgotten now – no one has been buried in them for fifty years although local service clubs loyally decorate the headstones of Civil War veterans with plastic flowers every Memorial Day.

A traveler on lonely country highways sometimes encounters small monuments, little breast-high pinnacles of carved stone set on granite plinths and surrounded by iron chain or spike fences. Corn and bean fields crowd the stone monuments carved with the names of pioneer families that the Indians butchered near these places in the summer of 1862. Some of the stone memorials are almost inaccessible – there is a granite tablet to the memory of troops ambushed at Redwood Ferry half-hidden in the jungle-like undergrowth draping the muddy river bank. Near the Lower Agency, there are headstones littering fields and the vacant fields where the foundations of long-gone buildings are marked. A couple of ancient warehouses stand aloof from the asphalt county highway, remnants of the old Indian Agency. Farmhouses annexed part of the site for many years and some of the structures had a second life as granaries – I think that the State has erected a small visitor center on land acquired for the public in that place now and tried to restore a couple of the buildings. On a deserted country blacktop, a marble angel stands in front of a rough-hewn cross – this is where the pioneers in Milford Township were butchered. The Milford monument is located at a curve in the road and local kids used to park there and throw empty beer cans in the grassy ditch nearby.

At Birch Coulee and on a boulevard at New Ulm and at Fort Ridgely, there are big obelisks reaching as high into the sky as the steeples of the local Lutheran churches. On the ridge overlooking Morton, two such obelisks stand incongruously side by side among tall trees. One obelisks, slightly the shorter, commemorates the "Faithful Indians" who assisted settlers through dangers to safety. Another obelisk names the soldiers killed at Birch Coulee – that monument is capped with a jasper arrowhead pointing up at the pitiless heavens above. A few miles away, the memorial to the Schwandt family, names the women and children killed at that place, and calls them "Martyrs to Civilization." These larger and more floridly expressive monuments have proven embarrassing to the Minnesota Historical Society entrusted to their maintenance – the big obelisks are imperishable and bear inscriptions that are politically incorrect in profound ways. Accordingly, the visitor will find these obelisks and sculpted stone pillars accompanied by small, but emphatic modern plaques, denouncing the big commemorative monuments towering overhead. It is a kind of shrill dialogue – the enduring granite obelisks chiseled with names and Periclean sentiments and the small signs nearby yapping at them with beagle-like persistence and abusing the big monuments for their shabby grandiloquence, deceit and racism. I suppose that some future generation will install microchip transmitters in the sod at these places once drenched in blood. Electronic voices will inform visitors through their cell phones that both the stone obelisks and the corrective plaques footnoting them are equally wrong, that human savagery is ubiquitous and eternal, and that it does no good for anyone to remember such things, that they are best forgotten, and thus should perish from the earth.

In 1912, 8,500 pounds of granite were carved into a block bearing this legend: HERE WERE HANGED 38 SIOUX INDIANS – DECEMBER 26, 1862. The big stone was embedded next to a river-front street in Mankato. Of all the monuments to the Uprising, this brutal and laconic stone was, perhaps, the most effective. The letters hammered out of the rock were stark and the monument's form was graceless, heavy, awkward – it was like a hideous meteorite fallen from outer space. The big chunk of granite was stuck like a bone in the throat of the city. It was a scandal, a stumbling block. Native Americans found the monument offensive. On several occasions, AIM activists dowsed it in blood, or, at least, some sort of red, viscous substance. In 1971, exploiting as an excuse the construction of a new bridge in the vicinity, the City of Mankato had the Hanging Stone hauled away. City workers recalled the monument, lurking like a bad dream, in a storage lot near Sibley Park. Then, sometime after 1991, the discredited monument simply vanished. A decade later, a history class at Mankato State University tried to discover the location of the Hanging Stone. By that time, no one knew what had been done to it or where it had gone. Some said that the Hanging Stone had been ground into gravel and buried under the limestone bison now standing across from Mankato's Public Library in a little tract of shrubbery called Reconciliation Park. Others hinted that the Hanging Stone had been trucked to the Standing Rock Reservation in North Dakota and was drowned in the turbid waters of the Missouri River reservoir or, perhaps, buried beneath the monument erected by the tribe on the place where Sitting Bull was murdered. But no one knows for sure and the inquiries of the University students and their professor were ultimately fruitless.

The Hanging Stone marked the place where local people recalled the execution scaffold as standing. On December 26, 1862, 1400 Federal soldiers stood ranked around the scaffold. The Indians were hooded and chanted their death songs as they were positioned on the gallows. There were three drum rolls. On the third roll, a man named William Duley, cut the rope holding the suspended scaffold, dropping the condemned men to their death. Duley was a survivor of the Lake Shetek massacre, the killing of several families of pioneers in a miserable little marsh that came to be known as Slaughter Slough. When the platform fell, an eyewitness said that the assembled crowd of civilians gave "one, not loud, but prolonged cheer...and, then, all were silent and earnest."

Many years ago, I took my wife and children to a powwow in Mankato in a place called Land of Memories Park. The park is located where the Blue Earth River courses through ravines and joins with the Minnesota. It is a leafy place that seems somehow boxed-in, river bluffs huddle around the confluence of the two rivers and the land is low, sodden, frequently flooded.

I think the powwow was intertribal. Some drum circles were competing for local honors and there were a lot of RVs and tents pitched in the campground nearby. Vendors had set up booths selling fry-bread drenched with honey or dusted with powdered sugar, turquoise jewelry, feathered regalia, and leather goods. Needless to say, alcohol and beer was forbidden. Flocks of scuffed Harleys came and went. People had brought lawn chairs and lounged around the place where the grass dancers had marked the place for the festivities. Fancy dancers whirled and flashed their plumage. Fat old men wearing sunglasses pounded relentlessly at the drums. Someone called for an honor dance and veteran's groups gathered with their banners and American flags. The warriors shuffled in slow circles while the drums kept the beat. A woman pointed up at the sky. High overhead, several eagles had gathered to hover over the park. The eagles rode the thermals in graceful looping circles that mirrored the dance on the ground beneath them. I have no idea what this meant. But I saw the eagles. I saw them with my own eyes.

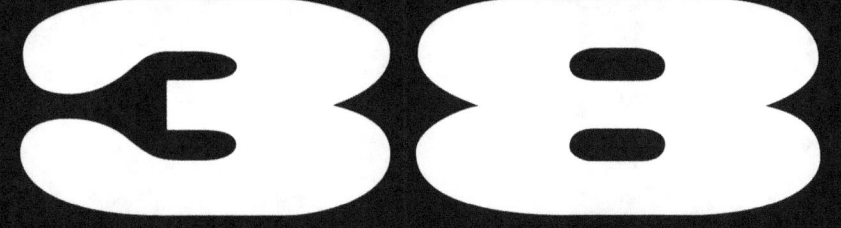

1

Bad companions were the death of me. My mother said that I should stay with the cut-hairs and keep among those in the houses built with sticks. She told me that her grandfather had been a Frenchman and that it was only by accident that we had come to live among these wild people. She said that I should go to school and learn to read and write and follow the way of the farmers who grew corn and squash beside their huts. Last year, when some of the other boys went away to camp and hunt the buffalo, my mother said that I should stay at home and there was a quarrel among my uncles until, at last, one of them said that I was too small for the long trek and that there would be no harm if I waited another year before joining the chase.

It was lonely among the girls and smaller boys at the Mission school. Sometimes, I ran away to fish in the river with the boys whose fathers had forbidden them to attend school. We took waterfowl from the shallows and killed squirrels and gophers with our arrows. Once, a badger chased us. We cooked what we killed in the clearings that floods had made along the river. By midsummer, the deadfall and driftwood heaped where the flood had left it was dry as tinder and we built fires from it. Sometimes, the boys who had gone on hunts took embers and burned their wrists and forearms to show their courage. The boys said that I should quit school and go with them every day to fish and chase game in the woods. Once, I burned my wrist also with a glowing twig and, when the tears, came into my eyes, I said that it was because of the smoke from the fire.

On the Sunday before the shooting began, I went to church with the other cut-hairs and saw the head-man there, also with his hymnal and frock coat split into tails under his bottom. After services, we sat on the porch of the stick-built house and smoked. My mother went away to wash clothing in the river and, then, we heard the shooting.

Two boys that I knew from killing squirrels came up from the valley. They told me to come and see a colt that they had found. I saw smoke coming from the ridge where the traders kept their flour and beans in the big stone house. The woods by the river were full of men and boys coming and going. We went along a path to where some boys were holding a colt with a rope around his neck. The colt danced away from the boys and they pulled on him and laughed. A horse all prickly with arrows was lying dead by the ferry-boat and there was a white man leaning his shoulders against a tree with blood all over his face. I heard a woman crying in the thicket. Someone said that the woman was the white man's wife and that the men and boys were all going into where she lay in the sumac with a wound in her belly and thigh. Someone said that I should go into her also and so I crept through the bushes to where the boys were holding her down. I did other bad things as well and, now, I must be hanged for this.

2

It was very fine to go out in the morning, in feathers and paint, all attired for war. It was good to feel the strong pony beneath me and to be in the company of men. It was good to go to war with the sun shining and not have to skulk about in the darkness, stealing chunks of meat from their smokehouses or assasinating chickens.

At first, they were easy to kill. The Dutchmen, in particular, had no stomach for a fight and would run away without protecting their women. Then, we would send boys to hunt them down and drive sharp sticks between their shoulder-blades. In this way, the older men could enjoy their women and, then, cut them apart while the boys stabbed the Dutchmen and made them die in their fields. Then, we set everything ablaze and burnt up the children if there were any still alive and went riding, swift as the wind, to the next place and the next. In two days, we killed them from morning to night, and I saw only two of our men wounded, one of them bit on the ear by a woman that he was raping and the other lit afire when he became drunk and ventured too close to a cabin that we were burning.

It was different later. All the bands were killing the white men and pretty soon the country was empty. Then, when we came up their farms or the settlements where they had lived, the people were gone or already dead with the women rotting in the doorways and ruined so that not even the pigs running wild would eat them. There was nothing to do but shoot arrows into the corpses and ride fast across the prairie in the hope that we might find some children that had been spared by the first band or a caravan of white people with their wagons and oxen fleeing to the soldier's house near the river. Once, we came upon just such a group of white people and it was a fine killing spree, but, then, after that, there was no one left, just ruins with chimneys standing in the ashes and the sad sound of their cows crying to be milked in the woods.

Then, the soldiers came. They would not fight us like men. They stood close together and would not duel and, when you rode against them, their guns would bark at you all together so that our men fell down as if blown to the earth by a great, hot wind. Their wagon guns knocked horsemen down from farther away than our rifles could shoot and, after several weeks, when we went back to camp to enjoy the captives that we had taken, the head men had removed them from our tipis and put them under their protection because they said that this war would be lost and that anyone who had molested a white woman would surely be hanged and that it was better to protect them and, even, give them berries and the best cuts of meat so that they might forgive us for what had happened earlier.

The soldiers took me on the road to the pipestone quarries. Two of my brothers gave me whiskey and, when I was drunk, they surrendered me to the white men. Then, I was put in leg-irons. The women that I had molested did not forgive me and so I am to be hanged.

3

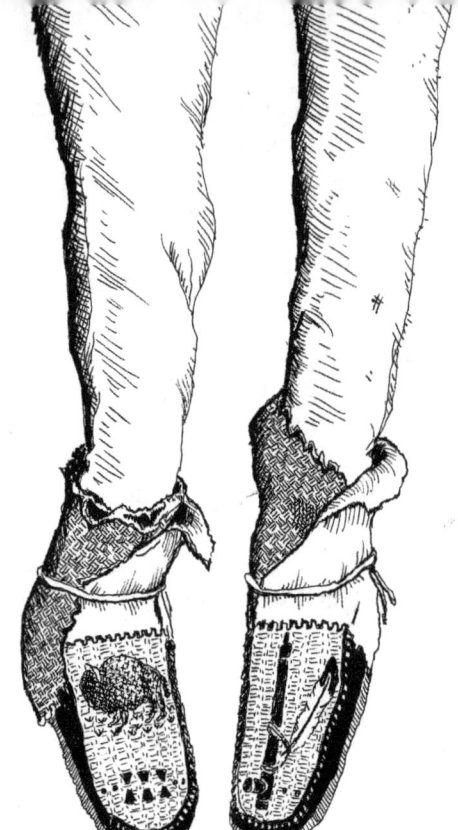

I will be hanged on account of the Dutchman's gun. Since the gun was never fired but once in anger, and, then, to knock down a boy from my village, I am to be hanged for nothing.

Before dawn, in the hour when the birds sing, the men went away to fight at the soldier's house. The women said that the boys my age would be too reckless and would lose their lives by accident or for no good purpose and so we were forbidden to go to the battle. When the sun was high, those of us remaining in the camp took some ponies and rode out along the hills overlooking the river. I think there were eleven or twelve of us. We looked at the dead white people lying in their fields and beside the ashes of their cabins. On the trail to the ferry, we saw more dead people, mostly soldiers rotting in their blue coats.

One of the boys said that he had heard that the missionaries were fleeing across the prairie north of the river. We crossed at the ford and followed the game trails up the ravine to the open country. Far away, moving slowly in the deep grass, we saw black specks, like ants, moving under the hot, blue sky. At first, we thought it might be soldiers and so we dismounted and went on our hands and knees to the crest of a hill to look down upon the white man's road and, beyond that dirt track, to the marshy country where the group was moving.

It was the missionaries trudging along behind wagons heavily loaded with children and baggage. A small group of cut-hairs walked ahead of them, trampling down the tall grass and finding the best places for the wagons to go among the ponds and wet lands. They were afraid of ambush along the road and so had gone onto the prairie but their way was slow because of the marshes where the redwinged blackbirds and grouse were starting up under their slow advance.

We left the horses in a wooded draw where there was water and crept through the grass and sloshed through the black-water sloughs until we were ahead of the missionaries. We had spears and clubs and whispered together about whether we should attack and kill them all. Someone remembered how a missionary had been kind to his mother during a cold month when there was sickness in the village and so we decided to let them escape.

Later on the road, we met a Dutchman with his family. He shot one of us in the belly and, then, we took away his gun. A couple of other boys tried to use the gun, but couldn't get it to fire. We didn't molest the Dutchman, even though he had killed one of us. I heard that some other war party killed him and the others traveling with him later that afternoon.

Later, after the fighting was done, a white soldier saw me carrying the Dutchman's gun. Then, the other boys lied about me and so I must die.

4

I have been a beggar and a lay-about and so it will be a relief to die. But it was not always so...

Once I was a respectable man with two wives, children, and many fine horses. Sickness came to our village and most of us died. I believed in the gods of our people and so I danced against the sickness until I was too weak to continue, but it was for nothing. My wives and children died with the blister fever and I was left with this face that you now see. We died alone in my tipi. The people who survived the fever were afraid to come to our aid and I was too weak to attend to the dead so the maggots ate my wives and children.

After I recovered, I walked on the Federal Road to the towns built by the white men. I became a good-for-nothing and a drunk. I begged on the porches of public houses and at the back doors of farms. I made firewood for the white men and carried their water. I lived with their swine and cattle, sleeping on dirty straw, far away from my people.

A few weeks before the fighting along the river, I learned that my aunt was dying and so I went to say goodbye to her. I walked back along the Federal Road which had become much bigger and broader and was crowded with teamsters with their rigs. I slept in the ditches and took eggs from under roosting chickens to eat and, several times, farmers with bird guns fired buckshot at me.

A few miles from the land reserved for us, I stopped to beg at a farmhouse. I knew the people that lived there from the time before the blister fever. Two women were at the house. Their man had gone away to fight the grey-coat soldiers. A fourteen-year old boy also lived with them and tended to the animals. I asked for food, mostly using gestures since I didn't want them to insult or admonish me. When the white people knew that I could speak their language, they called me names or asked questions that I didn't want to answer or tried to bargain with me and all of these things were unpleasant. After a few minutes, one of the women gave me an old piece of beef full of gristle. It was meat that a dog would reject. The woman spoke in front of me because she thought that I did not understand: "That one," she said, "is even too lazy to steal."

Several days later, the fighting at the Agency began. I borrowed one of my uncles war-club and a sharp knife and went back to see those women. I will be hanged for what I did and this is a relief to me.

5

After the killing stopped, we had no food. Because of the war, we had neglected the summer hunt and had failed to lay-in provisions for the hungry months. I had lost everything in the fighting and no longer had a pony or, even, a firearm. Many years ago, my great-grandfathers took buffalo and elk by ambushing them on the open prairie. My great-grandfathers had known how to make snares of willow and birch to trap rabbits and squirrels. But I had never hunted except on horseback and with a rifle and so I was unsuccessful in taking any game. In the end, I ate frogs and swallowed the green scum off ponds and, at last, when I could no longer bear the hunger, I went to the soldier's house and surrendered.

An old white man with a great round beard on his jaws asked me what part I had taken in the fighting. I told him that I had done only what a man and a soldier would do. He asked me again and so I said that I had fought two days in the village and saw the houses all burnt to the ground. I told him that I had led war parties against the soldier's house as well. I did not tell him that I had been at the fight where the warriors came from the ravine at dawn and cut down many soldiers camped nearby. I knew that the soldiers were ashamed about what had happened in that battle and that they were apt to treat a man harshly if he had led warriors against them in that place. The old white man said that I must be a gallant fellow and released me into the encampment where the other prisoners were confined.

A few days later, four soldiers with rifles came and marched me to a little log cabin on the hilltop. Inside the cabin, there was a pot-bellied stove that wheezed like an old dog, a squint-eyed interpreter who made his words more like a *metis* Frenchman than like one of our people, and many soldiers scribbling in big books like the ledgers in which traders maintained their records of account. Two women brought in a little white boy whose arm was in a sling made of bandages. The little boy spoke and, then, began to weep. A woman wiped his eyes. Then, he pointed at me with his free hand. I denied what he had said when it was translated for me, but it was no good. One of the white men told me that I was condemned to hang. I said: "What justice is this, to murder a man on the word of a boy not yet five years old?"

There were others awaiting trial, fettered along the wall of the cabin. Among them were some of my wife's people. They laughed to hear that I would be hanged. "You are not so proud now," they said to me. I said: "We will hang, all of us together." Then, the soldiers took me to the blacksmith who put these irons on my legs and I suppose I must wear them until I am hanged.

It's my mother's fault that I am now waiting to die. On the day that the war party went away to fight at the soldier's house, the men met before dawn. I was awake and went from my tipi to join them beside the embers of the fire. It was the hour when birds sing to rouse one another. The man who was to lead the attack said that there were many rifles in the fort. He said that the fort was defended by a wagon gun that could throw a metal ball as big as a man's head farther than a man can see. Some of the soldiers sang their death song. The war chief said that it would be a bright day with clear skies and that no one should be ashamed to die on such a day. My mother had come from the shadows and stood behind me and, when the war party went to the horse corral, she held me back. I fought against her but my uncle, who was among the soldiers, said that there would be other battles and that I should stay in the village with the other boys to protect the women in case the white men came unexpectedly.

We didn't remain in the village. Instead, when the sun was high, we took horses ourselves and rode out to find white farmers to kill. There were twelve of us and we rode wildly, without regard for the brambles and hills, and so, very soon, our ponies were all worn out and had to rest. While we were watering the horses among the swamps north of the river, someone said that soldiers were coming. We hid in the tall grass until we saw that it was not soldiers but missionaries running away from their church. We set an ambush for them, but things did not happen as we expected and so we left that place without molesting anyone and galloped along the Federal Road. For a few hours, the only white people that we saw were dead and rotted and some of them were half-eaten by their pigs or torn apart by wolves.

As we were arguing about whether to ride back to the village, a Dutchman with his cows and a wagon came down the lane. The Dutchman's women and children were huddled under blankets in the back of the wagon as if they were some kind of freight that he was carrying. Despite the heat, the women and children were shivering as if with cold and I saw the blankets that covered them trembling.

The Dutchmen knew a little of our language and spoke to us. He said: "You boys, what are you doing?" We didn't answer him, but parted so as to let the wagon and his cows pass between us on the narrow lane. Then, my cousin saw the Dutchman's gun and asked him for it. The Dutchman said that he would not give us the gun. My cousin tried to take it from him and was shot in the belly. We killed the Dutchman while he was trying to reload the weapon. We killed the rest of them and drove off the cattle. Then, we hid the gun because we were afraid of what the women in our village would say. We told the war chief that a soldier had killed my cousin.

In the hungry months after the fighting, we retrieved the gun from where it was hidden to hunt for game. A white man saw us with the gun and the soldiers came and, now, I will be hanged in the morning. I think if I had gone with the men to attack the soldier's house I would not now be waiting to die.

7

The people will need leaders after I have been hanged. It is no easy matter to guide the Lakotah. My only regret is that I can no longer help my people.

During the fighting, we took counsel each night. The young men and the soldiers' lodges would not follow the chiefs that had made pacts with the whites. War chiefs lead the counsel meetings and, I think, they made many bad decisions. A war chief is good for a day or two of raiding, or, perhaps, even a pitched battle, but an actual war, lasting more than a season, requires other skills and more deliberation.

I advised that the raids end and that we gather the fighting men from every village to make one great attack on the Dutchmen's town. I said that the town was scattered along the river and would be difficult to defend. If that town were destroyed, our men could sweep along the south side of the river and roll the white men back as far as St. Paul. We would not even have to fight. The white men would flee before us. If we burnt their town, they would have no stomach for war.

No one listened to me. Many of the young men who had gone to the buffalo hunt as far west as the Black Hills were returning to the war and they wanted their share of the spoils from raiding across the prairie. So we didn't gather forces for several days and, then, wasted our efforts on the Fort where there were blue-coat soldiers and wagon guns. I was not with the little group of men who tried to loot the outbuildings at the town but fled when it rained and made them wet.

We fought at the fort again and were repelled. The next morning, we lit the prairie on fire to make it seem that the fort had fallen. Then, at last, we gathered the soldiers' lodges and all the boys to make an attack on the town. It took a long time to get the men in one place and we did not advance on the town until mid-morning. We came from the west spreading out over the open ground and, at first, the white men ran away from us. A few of them hid in a wooden windmill and a brick house and fought very bravely. Instead of killing the men in the windmill and brick house, we charged around those buildings and, then, suffered many casualties from rifle-fire coming from behind us. Our assault broke into separate bands and they dispersed across too broad a front and, after an hour or so, the advantage was lost and we were scattered on all sides of the Dutchman's town so that it was hard to coordinate our efforts.

A hot west wind blew and, by mid-afternoon, most of the wooden buildings in the town were burning so that a great plume of smoke drifted down to the banks of the river. I spent several hours gathering men at the river for an attack from the west covered by the smoke. But before we were ready, thirty enemy charged through the haze and surprised us and my force scattered. Then, we went to ground, fighting from the burnt cellars and it was at this time that I saw the white man on his big horse ride wildly into our rifle fire so that he was killed and some of our fighters also when they tried to count coup on him.

This was the last battle where we attacked with strategy and for a purpose. We lost the fight in the Dutchmen's town and, from that time, I knew that the war could not be won.

I remember many guns around the place where the two roads crossed. All of them were being fired and the powder-smoke was like fog that rises from the snow when the day is too warm for the season. The white men were behind a heap of barrels blocking one of the roads and they were shooting at us. Other white men were in the houses, firing from the windows or from holes knocked through the stick walls. Some of the houses were on fire, but the white men remained in them, behind the walls and kept shooting at us even as the flames ran across their roof-tops. We crouched among the shacks and the outbuildings and lay on our bellies in the ash-pits where houses had been burnt down to their cellars and we shot our guns into the smoke, at the houses standing behind the beer-barrels and, all the time, there was a tremendous noise of men shouting that the enemy should come out from where they were hiding and fight face-to-face, bullets crashing into things and guns popping and banging and, always, the roar of the flames that were burning everywhere. So many bullets and bursts of bird-shot were flying across where the roads came together that if a dog were to run across that street, or, even, a rat it would be shot many times over before reaching shelter.

There was green hay in one of the stables and it burnt with a black, greasy smoke. The smoke was heavy and clung close to the ground and a number of us gathered behind it. We loaded our rifles and planned to make a charge through the smoke toward the side of the barricade of barrels heaped-up on the road. Just then, there was a great shout and one of our men came whirling and dancing through the smoke, shouting that the white men were attacking from between two flaming houses to the side of the place where the roads met. I saw a fine white horse gallop forward. The man on the horse was waving a revolver in circles and shouting something. The horse leaped high over a barrel that had rolled into the street and, then, reared up to kick with its hooves at some burning rubbish that had fallen across its way from one of the houses. When the horse showed us its breast and belly we all shot our guns and the animal pitched backward. The man tried to stand up but bullets were flying all about him. He crouched for a moment and stretched out his hand with his pistol. Then, he fell backward behind the body of the horse.

I shot at this white man, but no one else. I did not go with the war parties that killed the settlers. I was at the soldier's house on both days that we fought there but never came close enough to the fort to fire my gun. There was thunder and rain on the first day that we fought at the Dutchmen's town. It is bad medicine for me to make war when there is thunder in the sky and so I stayed in my lodge on that day. I have been told that Captain Dodd was the white man killed on the second afternoon of fighting in the Dutchmen's town and, although I saw him fall, there is no way of knowing whether he was hit by my bullet, or by the bullets of dozens of other men fighting there, or, perhaps, even shot down by the guns that the white men were firing at us. Other accusations against me are lies and it seems wrong that I should die for defending myself in combat.

I am glad that the prison is dark. There are others always around me, fettered very close to this corner where I hide, and I do not want them to see that my face is always wet with weeping. The food is not good and I am very lonely among these older, bad men. My family is large and I am the eldest son and have never been apart from my mother and my brothers and little sisters for such a long time and it is the homesickness that makes me sad and causes my tears, not the thought that I am to be hanged. I am so very, very sad with homesickness.

We lived near the Mission and my father was friends with the pastors at the church. I attended the Mission School and learned to read and write and had my hair cut like a white man. My father was corrupted by the white man's whiskey and, one day, while riding his horse drunk, he fell and broke his back. Then, he could not move and, after a while, died, wrapped in his foul-smelling buffalo-skin blanket and my mother let the pastors bury him like a white man, in the soil, for the worms to eat. Then, I was father to my smaller brothers and my little sisters and I left school to help support the family by working for wages on the farm that some of our people had started. I worked in the hot sun pulling weeds and hoeing in the dirt and cutting up the sod to make gardens and, in the evening, I came home to our tipi where my mother served me supper first so that I could eat the choicest meat and vegetables before the others took their portion. We were all close together in our tipi and the little girls gathered flowers for me during the day and crowned me with them when I arrived home at night. On Sunday, when we did not work, we went down to the river and tried to catch fish and my smaller brothers whittled lances and used them to try to stab the fat, barbel-headed catfish where they wallowed in the shallows. We went among the sumac thickets and gathered berries. My little sisters liked berries and their lips were sweet and colored with them when we went through the brush taking the berries from where they were growing: there were black berries and boysenberries and currants and raspberries that grew close to the ground in tangles of vine that ripped at your ankles and strawberries in patches under the mulch-grass in the white man's gardens -- we went there in the twilight to steal them sometimes -- and gooseberries also. What I would give now to hear my little sisters laughing in the dusk as they snatched berries from the flowering vines! How fine it was to be all together and to know my mother would be waiting for us at home, her eyes and cheeks glowing red with the color of the embers dying in our cook-fire!

I was the eldest son and so accustomed to being obeyed by the younger children and so I was not happy to be in the company of the big, rough men who ordered me around. The big, rough men are soldiers and, I always thought it was brave thing to be a soldier, although ignorant as well. Now, I have gone with those men and killed white people with them and I see that it is no harder to kill a white woman or baby than it is to slaughter lambs or behead chickens. Killing people is the easiest of all things. It is not as hard as gripping a hoe that blisters the hand all day long. I hope I don't cry when I see my mother and little sisters before they hang me. I am almost happy to be hanged because I know that the white guards will let us see our loved ones for just a few minutes before we are killed and, at least, that will end this awful homesickness that now breaks my heart and wets my cheeks.

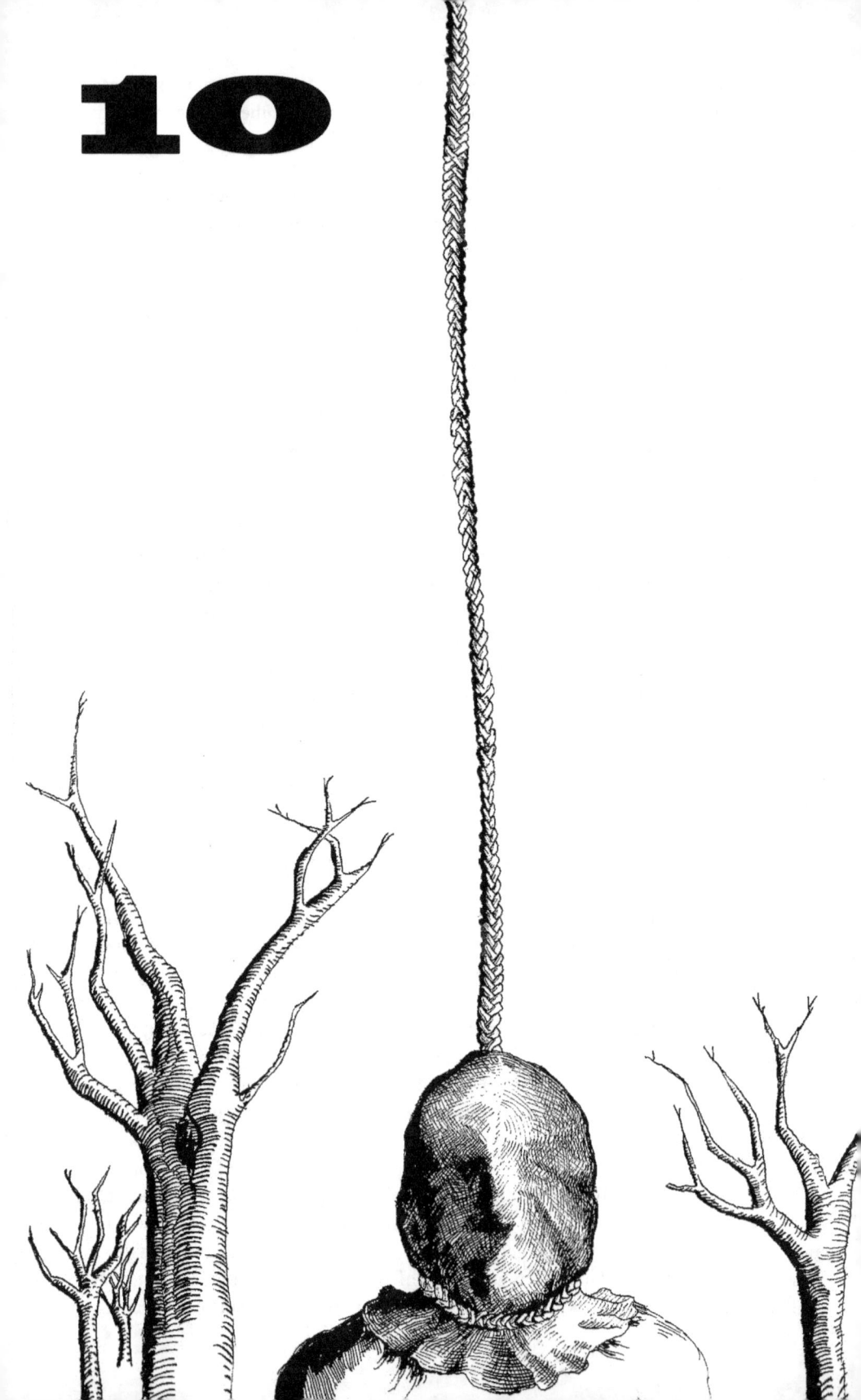

I am happy that I am the oldest to be hanged. The young men rage against the shackles and spit out the food, but I am quite content to sleep all day with my belly full of the white man's pork and flour. It is time for me to die: I have outlived my wives and all of my sons. The Black Robe has sprinkled water on me and said his words and so I am confident that I will see my wives and children again very soon.

I remember when I saw my first white man. Then, we lived up along the big river, in the little sandy streambeds where the sweet water oozed from the stone. There had been some sickness and we had taken the dead men into the thickets to be placed in trees or hidden the bodies in the small caves under the river-bluffs. After feasting in honor of the dead men, we went to race our ponies on the bare flats where the river flooded each year. A white man came on horse to watch us and we thought that he was a ghost. We thought that he was a walking corpse because the skin on his hands and face was pale and grey. He looked to me like some soft creature that lives under stones or fallen logs in the woods.

But I was not afraid and I became friends with the white man who was a trader and he was kind to me and showed me his ways. After awhile, he married one of my sisters and lived in a house built by piling square stones one atop the other. I learned the white man's language and went to his cities and, once, met the Great White Father in his town not a day's ride from the great sea. I counseled my people to make treaties with the white men and we used their guns and powder to kill many of our enemies, particularly the Chippewa so that we drove them completely from the Big Woods and, then, had those forests for ourselves in which to take game and collect berries. And, then, I was present with all the head men and government officials in their beaver hats and made my mark on the paper that sold our lands to the white men in exchange for the government money and the provisions, all to be distributed each year in the moon when the prairie grass is tall enough to pasture our horses.

For several years, life was good and the payments were made but, then, the white men began fighting among themselves and the annuities were not distributed and our people began to starve. I said that the whites would keep their promises, but the men from the Soldiers' Lodge laughed and asked me how many children I would let starve before we killed the traders and took away the corn and flour and beef that they kept locked in the big brick houses. I said that the white men would keep their word. Then, someone laughed and said that I was a white man myself, or, not even, a white man but a white woman. So I said that I would come with them and kill the white men and their soft grey women and their baby boys that they dressed like little girls and that I was a Lakotah and would die with them. So that is what I have done.

11

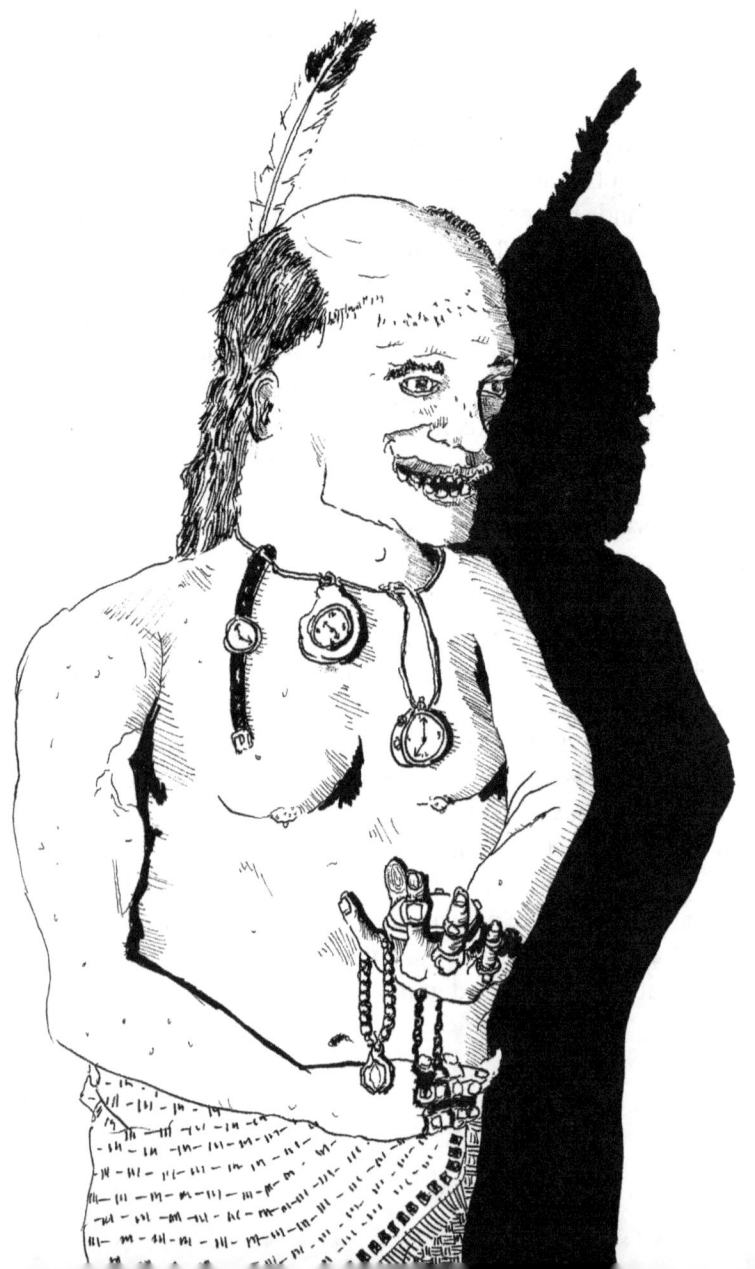

I saw white people killed but did not take part in their murder. I admit that my tent was filled with garments and utensils taken from their cabins and that I wore five or six of their time-pieces tied to a leather thong as a necklace at my throat. That I had these items in my possession shows only my love for the white man and how I wished to imitate him and, like him, own the hours and minutes . Of course, I am a thief, but it seems very harsh to hang me for stealing. We have all been undone by false promises. The general lied when he said that we could come in to the fort and be fed on boiled beef and that we would be pardoned so long as we had not harmed white women or children. It would have been better for me to have followed my cousins west across the big river and to the Black Hills which are sacred to our people and forever forbidden to these hardhearted and deceitful white men.

I was at the second fight at the soldier's house when the war chief was killed. I didn't fire my rifle that day. I slept late on the morning of the battle because my belly was all filled with potatos dug from gardens at a little settlement that the younger men had burned. We had found some preserved fruit and beer also and so there was feasting in our village; a few of the men molested the women that we had taken prisoners but I didn't participate, and, in fact, was drunk and vomiting in my tipi when those crimes occurred. I think it was Cut Nose who killed the baby that was crying so loudly that night and keeping us all awake when we were to be resting for the fight in the morning. I had no part in any of those things.

The soldier's lodges built campfires in the shady coulee that slanted downhill to the river from the bluffs where the fort was built. There were willow trees growing along the stream-bed and a little creek danced down the shady ravine, skipping over the stony places so that the place was cool with the sound of cascading water. The women came with baskets of food and they led pigs and calves uphill, along the creek so that they could butcher them and roast the meat close to where our men were firing at the soldiers in the fort. There were many women and children in the ravine, just beyond the range of the wagon-guns in the soldier's house, and the smell of roasting corn was fragrant among the trees and underbrush.

I joined one attack. We swarmed out of the ravine toward the stone sheds and the long barracks on the ridge overlooking the coulee. It was exciting to run as fast as I could toward the white clouds of smoke heaped like snow-drifts under the eaves of the buildings. The guns flamed there and our men shouted and, from the corner of my eye, I saw some of them drop heavily into the grass and that only increased my excitement and made me run faster. Then, the rotten cannon balls burst in the air and six or more men fell down all at once, none of them killed, but all ripped and torn, with great fistfuls of flesh scooped from their faces and torsos, and, when I saw how they had been wounded, with holes in their bodies that could not possibly heal, I was very afraid. I fell onto my belly and crawled nose-down through the grass, inhaling gnats and pelted by the grasshoppers splashing around me. You see, I was not afraid of dying, but the thought of having a wound like those made by the rotten cannon shot made me sick to my stomach. I reached the shelter of the ravine and rolled on my side down into the slough of dead leaves and decided that I would fight no more. I joined the women and roasted a pig and, later, the war chief was killed. Then, we knew that the battle was lost and we went back to our village.

12

When the food became scarce, I made a dog travois and went with my wife and children away from the Yellow Medicine Agency. My mother's people distrusted the white men and would not stay anywhere near their stick houses and gardens. They believed that the old ways were best and avoided even the traders with their blankets and pots. I knew that my mother's people lived west of the pipestone quarries where there were lakes white as snow with water-fowl and I thought that there would be food in their village, or, at least, game nearby to be taken.

My mother's people were poor, but they had smoked meat and good ponies to hunt along the Buffalo Ridge where it is always windy and hot. We stayed with them throughout the summer until the heat broke and the sumac leaves became bright as spilled blood. Then, I traded a white man's knife that I owned for a pony and set my wife to manage the dog travois and, in this way, returned with my family across the prairie to Yellow Medicine.

Of course, I had heard about the fighting, but I took no part. I saw some corpses lying in the grass but the birds and wolves had been at them and I couldn't tell if they were white people or Indians. Much of the country was deserted, it seemed, and we passed cabins that had been abandoned with the clothing that their women had been washing still pinned to the lines, but now all tattered and grey with dust. We saw more corpses along the Federal Road but they were just bundles of rags with hair still stuck to the skull-bones.

The Agency had been burned and my village had been struck so that only the tipi rings remained. We kept walking until we heard gunfire. It was a grey, moist day, heavy with dark club-shaped clouds and so, at first, I thought the booming sound was thunder approaching with a storm. We hurried into the shade of a wooded ravine and found that it was filled with our men firing their guns into a little, tattered encampment of soldiers. Some of the men told us that the soldiers had been burying bodies and that they had camped much closer than a rifle-shot to the ravine so that they would have water nearby. The encampment was a bad place to bivouac and, when I looked over the edge of the coulee, I could see their tents all torn with shot and their wagons whittled down by our bullets so close that I could have thrown a stone among them. I didn't have a gun, but watched the fight for awhile. Then, another column of soldiers came and threw some exploding shot among us and that is how my forearm was broken.

When my wound didn't heal, I came into the soldier's house to be treated. Then, I was put in chains and dragged into a cabin where many white men were writing as quickly as they could move their hands. My name is Hole-in-the-Day, but I was accused of crimes committed by Hole-in-the-Sky. Hole-in-the-Sky is a worthless fellow (he is my sister-in-law's cousin) and I know that he has fled west almost to the Yellowstone. A white woman with scars all over her face and chest pointed her finger at me and I was asked my name. I said Hole-in-the-Day and, then, the Judge said that I would have to be hanged for what I was supposed to have done. I will not speak my name in Lakotah because it would sound very much to you like Hole-in-the-Sky, but I am not that man and have harmed no one

I suppose all of us look alike to them and so I will be hanged for another man's crimes.

13

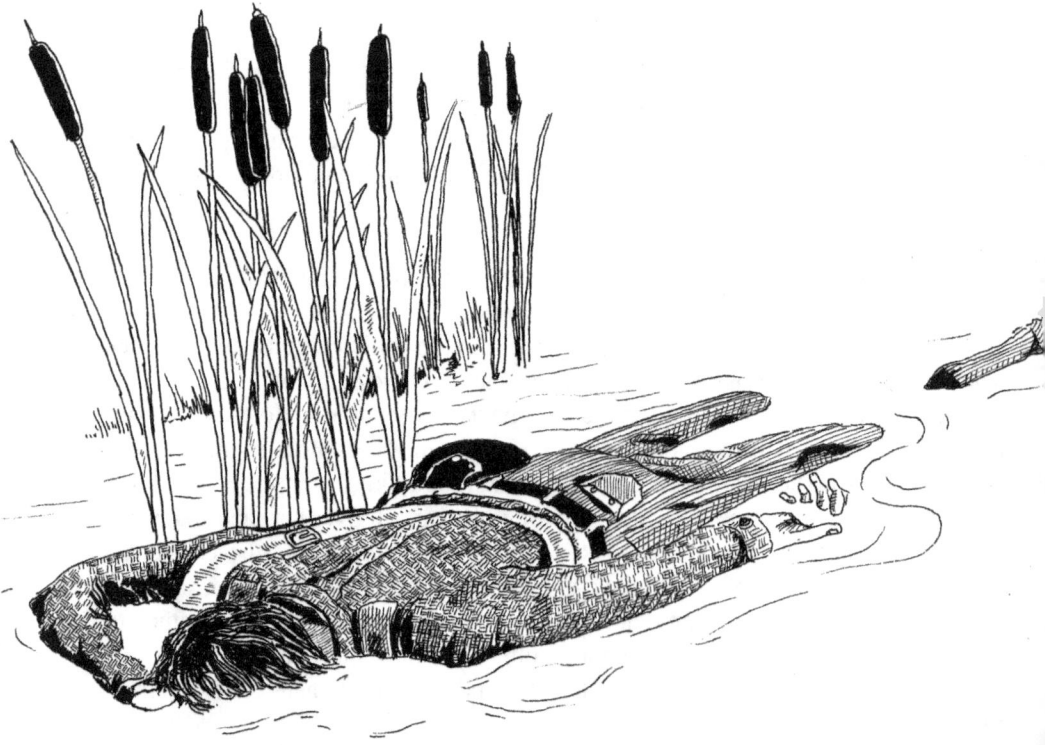

All of the others wanted to go raiding, but I said that we should stay home and wait for the soldiers to restore order. My mother said that much was being done in haste that would later be regretted and she told the old women to get switches and sticks to defend the pony corral so that the boys would not sneak away from the village. Many of the boys were angry, or professed anger, but I think that most of us were relieved that we didn't have to go away to the war.

My cousins said that we should go fishing and so we walked down to the ferry. We saw the dead soldiers lying where the river had pushed them and the smell made me sick. Then, a group of boys leading ponies came down to the water and I asked them where they had found the horses. "The old grannies fell asleep," the boys said. The old women had been awake from the hour before dawn when the men left the village to fight at the soldier's house and the hot sun shining through the trees made them sleepy and, soon enough, the boys said, they were snoring in the shade by the pony corral.

I said that I wanted to go back to the village but my cousins dragged me along and, once we had splashed across the river, there was no returning.

We found some cut-hairs leading the missionaries across the prairie. The other boys wanted to ambush them, but I said that this would be a very great crime and a sin against God. When the boys lifted their war clubs, I restrained them and so, after some quarreling, we agreed to let the missionaries continue on their way and we did not show ourselves. I crawled on my belly through the swamp with the red-winged blackbirds cursing at me and, hidden among the reeds, I saw the shadow-catcher with his box take their likeness as they sat resting among their wagons on blankets cast down upon the thick, green grass. The light flashed like the muzzle of a bird gun and the people sat blinking in the direction of that fire and, then, the man with the shadow-catcher box waved to them that they could commence moving again and I saw the cut-hairs and the missionaries all stretching their legs and arms as if they had just awakened from a long winter's nap. I wanted to keep crawling on my belly until I was safe among them, but my cousin restrained me and so we went back to horses and rode away.

Later, we came upon a Dutchman. He was lost and asked us for directions. When I tried to help him on his way, he threatened us with his gun and, then, before I could I stop them, the boys charged at him and he killed one of us before we could take his weapon away. I was comforting the boy who the Dutchmen had shot when the rest of it occurred and I swear that I did not lift my hand against any white man that day, or any other day.

When the soldiers called for us to come into their camp, I told the boys we should give them the Dutchman's gun. We went to where it was hidden and I was carrying the weapon so that we could surrender it to the soldiers when the horsemen came and captured us. There was a misunderstanding about what we were doing. Then, others lied about me and, now, I am to be hanged although I am innocent of any wrongdoing.

14

The Black Robes told me that there was no prison-house so dark and deep but that the Lord Jesus didn't come to visit those wretches confined in that place. So I believed and found my dungeon less dark and dreary. I believed and the brick walls of the prison fell away and I found myself on the open prairie in early spring, when the grass is young and green and sometimes slick with the last wet snowfall and game was abundant and easy to track and all things were delightful to me.

You see, prison is easy to bear if you believe. Boiled beef gives plenty of nourishment for the belly and there are hard-tack biscuits as well and we are warm enough despite the cold of winter outside and the winds that howl about the fortress where we are confined. At first, I was afraid and angry and, like many of the men here, awoke drowned in sweat from night-terrors and, then, wept all day long and cursed the white man for decreeing that we all must hang. I fought against my fetters until my ankles and wrists were slick with blood and considered that I might even hack off an arm and foot so as to free myself from the chains. The presence of all the other condemned men was a burden to me: at night, they cried out or were coughing continuously and spitting and some had dysentery and other bowel complaints and so there was perpetual stench and uproar and the sound of men being sick. I thought to myself that it was a cruel thing to keep us confined so long and that it would be far better for us all to be taken to the gallows and killed as quickly as possible. Someone said that the Great Father in Washington was reviewing our trials and that we had a strong friend in Bishop Whipple and that many had been condemned to death on nothing more than rumor and surmise. For my own part, I held out no hope of pardon. I knew what I had done and understood that it was wrong and that I must die for the part that I played in the rebellion. Others who held out hope for forgiveness talked about that tediously all day and all night, but I kept silent since I knew my actions and thought it dishonorable to deny the things that I had done.

Then, the Great Father's order came and the condemned were separated from the saved which, for me, meant only that I was taken to a smaller, darker prison and more tightly bound. I imagined myself strangling at the end of a tether such as white men use to lead dogs and goats. I thought of my dead body corrupting in the mud the way that white men bury their dead and pictured my mouth and eyes all full of dirt. Then, I wept also and, in that despair, the Black Robes came and told me that if I believed I would be saved. They read from their book about other men who had been in prison and how the earth had shaken and knocked free their fetters so that the prisoners could escape, but, instead, they remained in their cells singing hymns. And, as I heard these words, a great light came into the gloom of our dungeon and I felt my fetters become light and airy as if they were gold bracelets such as rich white women wear and, then, I knew that I would dwell forever in heaven and that I should no longer be afraid.

My only concern is that I will be the only Lakotah who took the path of war in heaven and that the other Indians will all be Cut Hairs of the kind that I found contemptible and womanish when I was free. I am working hard to bring the Truth of Jesus and his love to the man chained to my left and the boy at my right. I tell them that we will stand together in Paradise and that Jesus will smoke the pipe of peace with us and, then, we will all ride free and wild over prairies that are alway green and among great herds of game that shall never fail.

It was a near thing. It is like being pierced by a bullet or a lance: the width of a little finger may mean the difference between life and death. That is what I think.

In the last fight, all the clans were gathered. No one had gone raiding or fled onto the western prairie to join the buffalo hunt. We were all together in one place because we knew that the Soldier's House had not fallen and the Dutchman's Town, although it was burnt to ashes, had kept its people alive, and the army was now coming against us, marching in blue columns a mile long and we understood in our hearts that if these soldiers were not repelled, they would hunt us the way boys chase and harry and kill muskrats. Their wagon guns would pelt us with rotten shot and we would be afraid and the war would be lost.

For a couple of days, our scouts followed the troops as they marched over the prairie. The weather was fine and autumn was in the air and the great army marched quietly, almost without raising any dust, an endless blue snake that wriggled over the hillocks and potholes startling deer and other small game in our direction. Horsemen went at the front, coursing like hunting dogs and, at the flanks, battalions ranged right and left, poking through the marshes or searching the gullies. Their flags seemed always on the verge of toppling forward and fluttering to the ground. In the distance, we could not hear the orders that the officers shouted or the men speaking to one another: the only sound that passed through the cool, clear air was a faint tinkling of harnesses and water bottles bumping against the buttons on rucksacks or the metal of their bayonets.

The army camped beside an oval pond that opened like an eye in the plain's brown grass. We saw six of their horseman break away from the main column and ride north to the line of trees marking the river bluffs and the ruins of the Yellow Medicine Agency. The sun went down and the horsemen returned with some burlap sacks stuffed with loot and, then, their campfires spread out around the lake, a flicker of orange and yellow encircling the dark spot that was the pond.

Before dawn, the greatest number of our men massed behind a ridge overlooking the lake and about two rifle-shots from their camp. A hundred of us crept through the high grass along the road to the Agency. Our plan was to mount a small attack from the direction of the Agency. The soldiers would wheel about to face our assault and turn their wagon guns in our direction and, as soon as the cannon were pointing at us, the greater part of our force would storm down upon them from the ridge at their rear.

I was lying in the tall weeds when someone whispered that wagons were coming toward us. White men normally are noisy, but these soldiers were silent and cautious not to make any sounds. We tried to hold our position and remain hidden but a wagon actually passed its wheel over one of our men hidden in the grass and, when he cried out, our plans were spoiled. The soldiers on the wagons shot at us and we cut them down but the force behind the ridge was scattered and not yet in place. A wave of blue coats came at us, firing in volleys and we were obliged to retreat, some of our men also killed along the highway. Our warriors behind the ridge did not attack. By the time, I reached the main force, our army was already melting away, each clan going its separate way across the deep grass of the prairie.

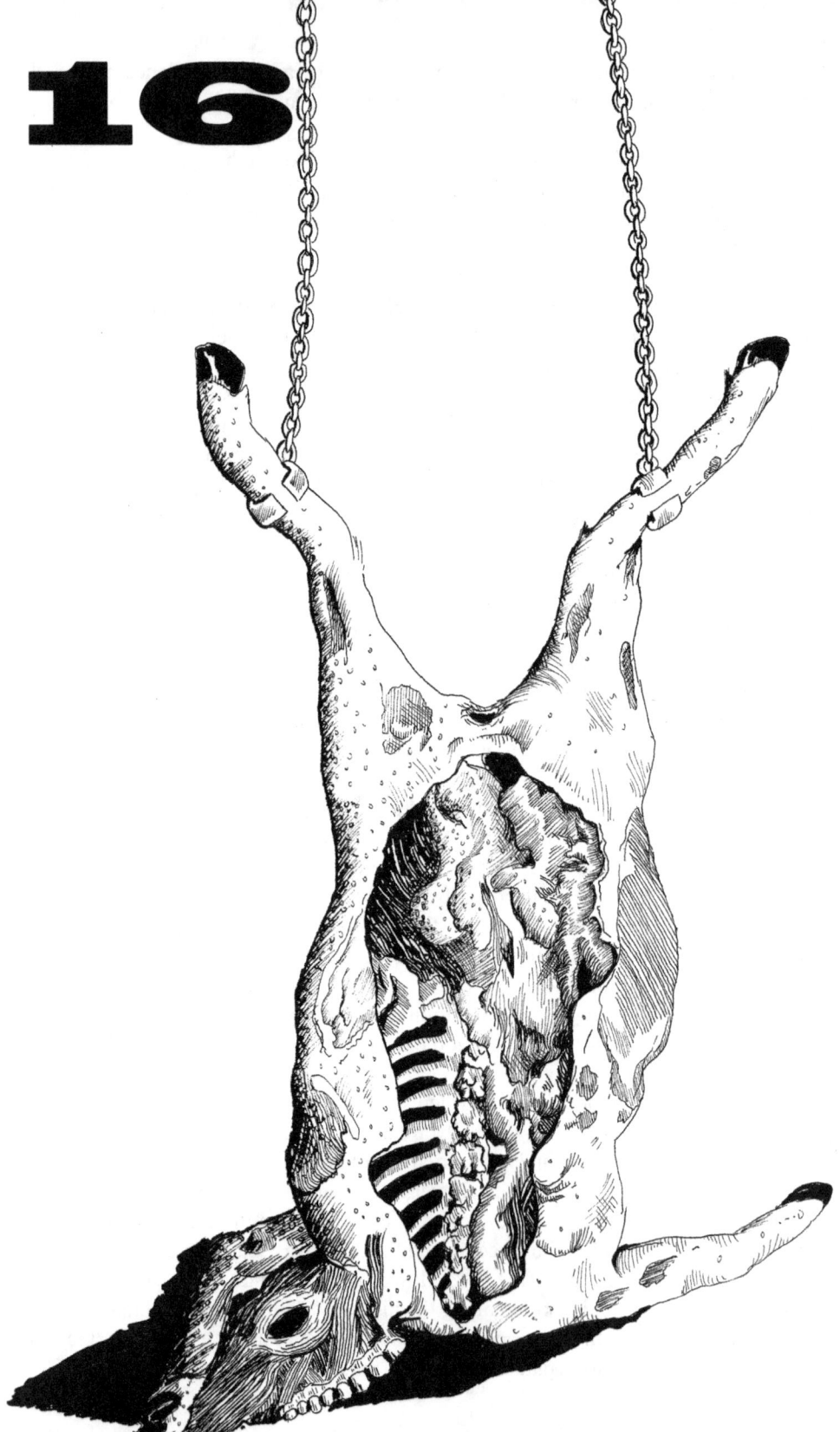

It seems very strange that these white animals have sentenced us to die for the way that we conducted this war against them. They seem to hold that war can be waged in a manner that is gentle or kind. The absurdity of their beliefs about war is staggering. How can war be anything but bloody, cruel, vicious, and destructive? Although there may be justice in the reasons for going to war, and justice, perhaps, in the objectives, there can be no justice in the fighting and killing. War is not war without killing and, yet, it seems, we are to be hanged precisely on this accusation. It makes no sense to me and I have made my head ache with trying to understand the white men's proclamations on this point and, yet, in the end, their words are nothing more than empty wind and noise.

Furthermore, I am not in the habit of taking lessons in justice from those whose entire lives are predicated upon injustice. I say this most assuredly: the white man's entire way of living is founded upon the most cruel injustice. I know this in my own heart and have felt it in my belly.

What kind of beast walls up food in a hoard and puts a price on flour and beans that must feed women and their little ones and, then, refuses to provide that food when the people are starving? What kind of monster insists upon payment from funds that the monster himself is withholding? No Indian would treat a dog with such cruelty and, yet, for the white people this kind of injustice as close to them as their own jugular vein.

Each year, annuity payments from Washington were to arrive around the time when the days are longest and a man can hunt until the night is half-done. But this time, the money was scattered by the fighting among the white men of the south and the white men of the north. The money was lost and did not come to us and, after the game around the river was exhausted and the big fish all taken from the waters, our people were very hungry. The children were starving and the nursing women so thin that their milk had no fat and no vigor and the littlest babies developed bloody flux and began to die. It was worse than the hungry moons in early spring when the meat from the fall hunt is mostly exhausted and you chew on old leather to keep away the hunger pangs because we had already chewed up the leather and eaten the last of the grease and berry mash and there was nothing else to sustain us.

We went in a delegation to the trader's house at the Agency and stood on his porch to demand that flour and beans be given to us on credit. The trader invited some of the men into his store and gave them tobacco and chicory coffee, but, he said that he was a servant to some other man and that the other man would not let him give us food on credit. More women and children starved and more babies died. We knew that the big brick warehouse was full of barrels of flour and beans and salt pork but the trader would not open the door for us. Some of us tried to break into the storage-house at night, but were driven away by the trader's dogs and, then, he hired half-breeds to patrol the agency with shotguns on their shoulders.

We pleaded for food again and were denied. Then, someone remembered that the Trader had said: "If the Lakotah are hungry, let them eat grass." Boys came from the Big Woods and said that they had killed white people and, the next day, we butchered the trader and ate his food.

17

Oh how I laughed to see the great and magnificent Cut Nose accused! Now, we will hang together and I will make certain that I do as well as he when it comes to dying. They say that we may be hooded when they hang us. I hope that this is not true. I will want to watch Cut Nose as his neck is stretched, although I suppose, he will not even favor me with his glance.

I am related to him somehow. He comes from my mother's people and, although once I tried to work out how we belonged to the same family, Cut Nose always ignored me and seemed to think it ignominious to be any kind of cousin or uncle to me. He was always so grand in the way that he strutted about, always at the forefront of the war party, always the first to dance and the longest to remain on the bent grass with the drums sounding. His horse corral was always full and, although he had several wives, he took the women of other men as well and no one dared accuse him.

Once, we went to war against our enemies who make their villages north of the Big Woods. There were twenty of us in the party and, of course, Cut Nose was our leader. In those days, I was a young man and as brave and reckless as the rest and I looked forward to proving myself in battle. We rode for five nights to reach the land claimed by our enemies. Along the way, I drank bad water and became very sick. Cut Nose said the war party should leave me behind, without my horse, near a spring in the Big Woods and that, when the fighting was over, the men would return and take me home. My brothers and cousins said that it would be dangerous to leave me alone when I was so sick and that I would surely fall prey to marauders or wolves that haunted that forest. They refused to leave me and, although Cut Nose denounced them bitterly, my friends remained at my side. We rested for a day and, then, when I was a little better, rode north again to find the Ojibway. Among the lakes, we came upon a hunting camp. Although I felt strong enough to take part in the fighting, Cut Nose called me a woman and beat me about the shoulders with his coup stick and, then, said that I should remain behind and hold the horses by their tethers while the other men fought. It was a good fight and some of our men had fine wounds bestowed upon them and others killed their enemies and took their scalps but I did not share in the glory. I was so ashamed that I challenged Cut Nose to a duel and hoped that he would kill me, but he only laughed in my face.

So it was very funny to come into the log cabin where the wood smoke burned your eyes and see the great Cut Nose with his shoulders flung back and his chin out-thrust declaring that he had never fired his gun except against the soldiers and, then, to see that little white boy, with his arm in a sling and hobbling about on crutches, come forth to make an accusation against the mighty war-chief. "He killed my mama," the boy said, standing no higher than Cut Nose's knee cap and the great war chief turned pale and rolled his eyes and said that the child lied, but now he is to be hanged because of that little boy and how I laughed from my belly to see him brought down by a baby standing no higher than his knee.

18

I was not at the first day of fighting at the soldier's house. With my sons and relations, I raided the settlements and killed the white farmers. This was a proper part of the war. We had no quarrel with the soldiers. The soldiers did not take our land or graze their beef cattle on our prairie; the soldiers did not put up fences or kill our game or break the sod. The soldiers were encamped at the Fort to protect the farmers. We thought that if the farmers were all dead, then, the soldiers would leave and the land would be restored to us.

Not all of the farmers died without fighting. Some of them took axes or pitchforks and died with those tools in their hands. I saw one of our boys shot through the throat by a farmer who was defending his wife and children. At several cabins, the men and boys fired their guns until they were out of the ammunition that they used to hunt grouse and duck. Bird shot scarred a few of our men. I was far to the north on the first day that our men attacked the soldier's house. I heard about the fighting at the Dutchmen's town but was raiding when that took place as well. The war chief said that we had killed enough settlers and so, early in the morning, we went with the others across the river to attack the fort. First, we would burn the fort, then, the Dutchmen's town.

No one was laughing or boasting when we walked through the gloomy woods to the Fort. I didn't hear anyone talking. Some boys tried to follow us and begged to hold our horses when we made the attack, but most of us went on foot since the soldier's house was close and we had heard that, on the first day, the wagon guns in the fort had destroyed many fine ponies. The boys chased us, but we threw stones at them and drove them back into the village where they would be safe. Some of the men sang their death song.

For most of the day, I crawled through the high grass and shot my rifle at the point where the wagon gun was rearing up on its hind legs when it fired and where the soldiers were hurrying to load and reload the black cannon. Once the shot set the tall grass on fire and we had to scramble back to the ravine with our feathered capes and moccasins burning. Later, a great number of us ran into the face of the gun, not pausing to duck or hide, and, then, rotten shot burst among us and whirling blades of metal the size of ravens swooped around us on all sides and I saw it cleaving through men with heavy axe-blows so that they collapsed all torn to pieces. It was an awful sight and I turned and ran away from the bellow of that gun. Before we could mount another attack, the war chief was killed. I was covered in blood and chunks of flesh and thought that I had been shot, but, later, found that it was wounds in other men that had sprayed gore on me during the attack.

Women had come from the village and they were roasting beef on spits in the ravine. I ate until my belly felt like it was going to burst. Then, I was very sick and vomited again and again. The sickness knocked me down and I could barely walk back to our village. I took to my tipi and remained too sick to stand, let alone to ride my ponies or, otherwise, go to war. Something had poisoned me during the feasting in the coulee at the Soldier's House and I was unable to leave my tent. My sleep was disturbed and I had many nightmares and the bad medicine sometimes burned so fiercely in me that I lost my vision and could not see. The troops captured me when I had become blind. I can see only well enough now to be hanged.

19

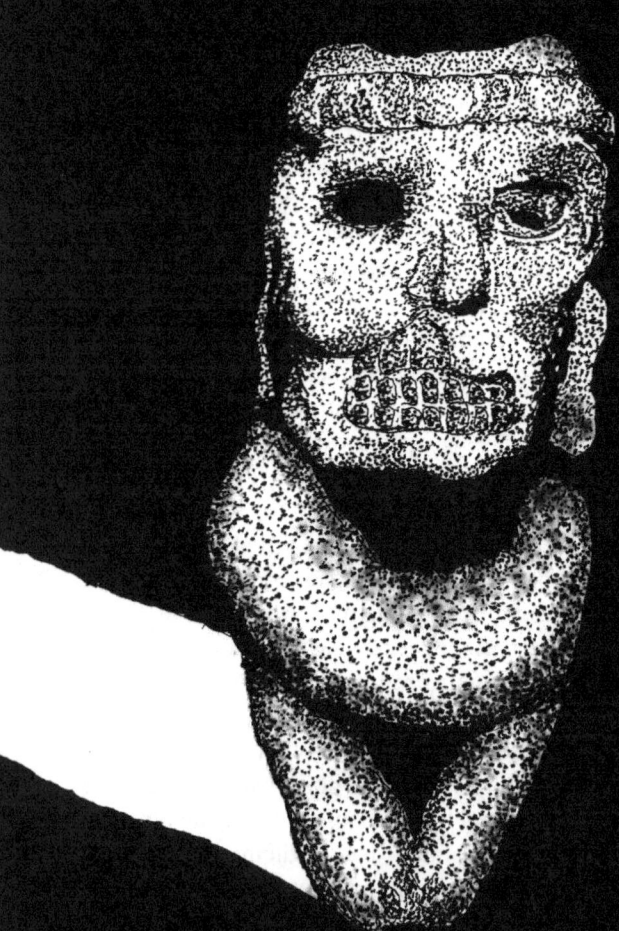

It is a hard thing to be hobbled by leg irons and kept in darkness with so many other men crowded closely about. There is nothing to do but eat when we are fed and, then, whisper together for a few minutes about the old days before the white man came and when the prairie that we rode our horses upon was ours to wander as we wished. The guards don't want us to talk and they strike at our faces with the stocks of their rifles and so we must keep our voices low and, after a while, the strain of whispering ends our conversations. So mostly we sleep away the hours and the days, dreaming through what remains of our lives.

In the last few days, I have been dreaming so vividly that it seems that I am having a vision like the kind that occurred when I was a young man and went alone into the dry country up to the high places where the eagles circled to earn my name. It is a vision like those that come from the emptiness in the body when the belly has not been fed and thirst has not been quenched and the hot sun burns down to make dreams walk and talk and, even, sing.

It seems that I see a white buffalo calf. The calf prances across a meadow that is bright with flowers. It is by the quarries where there are red slits in the grass where men are digging for pipestone and, beyond low cliffs of crystal the color of blood and a tiny stream that splashes down from above like a beam of light falling through an opening in the clouds.

I follow the calf and, by the waterfall, the calf vanishes and there is a young woman instead, bathing her slender body in the splashing stream. She is a limb of sleek, smooth willow in a cascade of silver. The young woman puts on her smock and springs up among the rocks, standing above me on the pinnacles of red crystal. When she beckons, I follow her and the way that looks so steep is really very easy, a kind of dancing on bright stone until I am at her side. Then, she leads me along a path where the grass is crushed and there are many ruts as if from the wagons of the white men and, at last, we see a town teeming with them that spreads as far as the eye can see with brick-built chimneys spewing smoke and, all about, mud and sewers and no green thing growing anywhere. Then, the White Buffalo Calf Woman reaches forward and parts the vision as if she were opening the flaps of a tent. She opens the white man's city and shows me that behind it, or inside, there is a vast prairie of grass as high as horse's fetlocks and buffalo in great herds. The white men have become buffalo and they swarm the prairie like mice, trotting up to us and lying on their sides so that we can better pierce their hearts with our feathered lances. So there is a great slaughter of buffalo and their meat is so abundant that we take only their tongues and the fatty humps from their shoulders and leave the rest for the ravens and crows.

The sun sets in a great hemorrhage of red and the dead buffalo become naked white people pecked and battered by the crows and the White Buffalo Calf Woman says to me: "See they are all dead and there are only Indians left living in the world." Then, she laughs and goes away and, when I open my eyes, and see that I am still chained in this prison, I weep and pray to dream once more.

20

Where white men are gathered, there is a great stench. The little villages that we burned were not so bad -- they were open to the wind that cleanses everything. But the larger places through which we were dragged in the icy rain are foul beyond endurance -- these places make me retch and gag. The fences and the walls and the brick and stick enclosures all trap the stink that they make and there are tanneries and slaughterhouses where heaps of offal are rotting and markets full of decomposing meat and vegetables and, sometimes, the sour, bitter smell of hops fermenting and grains turning to poison in their distilleries, and, on all sides, there are trenches full of night-soil and, everywhere, smoke from fires burning the most foul stuff imaginable and this whole rotting sewer stretches for miles in all directions and is packed with white people whose clothes are caked onto their bodies like filth and whose skin smells of death and decay.

I am afraid that they will take us on their trains to those places that I have heard about, far to the east, where the white men are like locusts and have devoured everything that is green and spread their disease across the whole land. Some of the men confined here have said that they will starve themselves to death if we are taken farther away from our lands where there is sweet-grass and water that flows through something other than dirty pipes. For us, it doesn't matter for we will be hanged here or there, it doesn't matter because none of us will survive -- my concern, which keeps me awake at night, and which fills my days with worry, is for the rest of our people, the women and children, the men and boys who were not condemned, the rest of the Lakotah who will be alive when we are dead.

Take this message to my wife and say to her that I will die like a warrior and a soldier who fought bravely for my people and that I will do nothing dishonorable. And tell her that the white men will spare the women and children for they take pride in a particular kind of cruelty and degradation that they call mercy. They will spare our women and children while trying their utmost to convert them to beggars and paupers and prostitutes in the pig's sty of their cities. Tell my wife that when the stockade gates are opened and the people freed, she must go as quickly as possible by whatever means are available to the west, away from all white people. She must take my sons and my daughters and they must walk through the Big Woods and take game there and steal chickens and eggs from the settlers if necessary, but always walk and keep walking until they come to the Buffalo Ridge and, then, the pothole lakes and the Black Hills at last. It will be a long and weary road that they must travel and, perhaps, they will be tempted to go into the white men's forts or villages to trade or work for food, but this they must not do -- if they must deal with the white men it should be as thieves in the night and in no other way, for the whites corrupt and destroy any Indian who comes near. My wife knows that we have kin beyond the Bear Lodge where the Powder River flows down from the mountains and she should go and live among those people and raise my sons and daughters in accord with the old ways and traditions of our people. And, if the white men come to the Powder River, then, she should take counsel with the head men and all of the people should go across the mountains and take lands from the Crow and Blackfeet, but, under no circumstance, should they live in any place where the smoke from a white man's chimney is visible or where they are gouging the earth to take the gold stones or within the sound of their train whistles that bellow in the night like demons. I have spoken: these are my final words.

21

I agree that the white men are cruel beyond measure and savage, but it is the rage of a wild beast, the fury of a mindless animal and nothing purposeful. There is nothing human in their brutality -- no premeditation, no objective or purpose directed toward the future. You see, I am not willing to ascribe those motives to them that others whisper about here in this prison house. What is the motivation in a wounded buffalo that gores a horseman or a cyclone sweeping across the prairie?

There are some that recall that day at Traverse when the soldiers marched down from the Fort where the rivers come together and there were men in black frock coats with tails split like the tongues of serpents and red, white, and blue flags were nailed to all the trees. The troops had built a bower of branches cut from the trees along the river and the leaves were still green and unwithered and I recall that underneath that shelter from the sun, ants and little green worms drizzled down from the foliage above. The papers that we signed were in that green shadow and I recall the sheets that color, like the pale grass that comes up after the last snow has melted. We all put our marks on the paper, which was scratchy under our pens, and, then, shook hands with the men in the black coats. Then, some soldiers put their mouths to metal cups in snakes of brass and there were loud sounds of the kind that they accounted as music. We cooked whole buffalo on spits and gave them an exhibition of our horsemanship and the hooves of our swift ponies thundered over the prairie.

Some say that they planned that very day, when we made the treaty with them, to take away our lands. I don't agree. To ascribe to them such foresight and planning would be to treat them as men with rational minds and hearts and, as far as I can see, they are not men at all but mere monsters of cruelty.

Others say that the annuity was not paid to goad us into this disastrous war and, then, defeat us and scatter us across the prairie and take away the lands promised to us along the river. But I am unwilling to believe this either. They are so vicious and warlike that they even fight among themselves and everyone knows that there is a great war far away in which they are perishing each day by the tens of thousands, all dying at the hands of one another. You see, in the midst of this war, their agreements with us were a very small thing and easily forgotten and it was a matter of negligence, carelessness, I think, that caused them to forget to pay us the money that we required to buy food for our families. They starved our women and little ones out of nothing more than carelessness, because they had forgotten about their "red brothers", as they had named us, living along the river in the camps that they allowed to us after the treaty. And that is a thing far worse, than intentional cruelty, I think: to be forgotten, to be starved to death out of negligence, and, then, when forced into war, to be captured like this and treated as criminals and, finally, hanged like dogs

It is a bad world that these white brutes inhabit and I will be glad to be out of it.

22

In this world, nothing is certain. Yet, I am as sure as possible that I will not be hanged. One of our number will be excused from the gallows and everyone agrees that I must be the man.

First, it is true that I took no part in the fighting against the white men. When the young men told the war chiefs to rise up and kill all the whites and cut hairs, I was secretly afraid for my own safety. Although I have lived in a tipi and followed our old ways for many years, I am half a cut hair myself. My mother died when I was an infant and I was raised at the Yellow Medicine Agency by the fur trader's wife -- a woman who is only partly Indian and, then, not from our tribe. I was taught to read and can write my name and I can reckon enough to cut a sharp deal in whiskey or pelts. When the killing began, I set my lodge apart from the village, kept away from the others, and amused myself hunting for grouse and rabbits. I returned to the clan -- I come from among Cut Nose's people -- only later, when the white vigilantes were roaming the hills and woods killing any Indians they encountered. Then, I thought it best to be with my father's family.

Second, I was convicted on lies told by Godfrey, the mulatto. Before I was called to the little cabin where our depositions were taken, Godfrey said that he was at all the major fights and that he could tell the white men those Indians who had been present. At that time, he thought the general who was acting as judge was condemning men for firing their guns at the soldiers and so he told the white men that he had been at the battles at the Fort on both days. Later, Godfrey understood that the Judge was mostly interested in learning about those who had taken part in raids against the settlers and so he told the Court that I was one of the men who killed the Eastlick family at Lake Shetek. None of the white people who survived that day recalled seeing my face, but Godfrey was influential with the Judge and I was condemned. Now, it is known that the first day of fighting at the Fort was the same day that the white settlers were killed at Lake Shetek and the two places are three sleeps distant from one another. Everything was written down and the White Father in Washington has commanded that the records be examined and I know that the transcript will neither lie nor fail me.

Only I (and you, my friend -- and you are already as much as a dead man) know that I probably deserve to die as much as any of the others in this prison. When I returned to live with my father's clan, Cut Nose had several prisoners, including two little white girls. The children were barely alive when I first saw them, lying in the filth and eating the slops that the dogs would not devour. One night when Cut Nose was gone to his mother's people, I went into his tipi and had my way with both of the little girls. They didn't resist me and, in fact, I thought I was doing them a kindness because I paid for their use with a couple handfuls of dried berries mixed with buffalo fat. I remember that they were cradling baby-dolls, all that remained of their life with the family that we had killed. Later, when we were obliged to flee from the soldiers, Cut Nose saw that the two little girls were foot-sore and could not keep up with our march and so he smashed out their brains and left them lying in the grass with the baby-dolls still clutched in their hands. So there are no witnesses against me and you speak only Lakotah so you can not tell anyone what I have said to me. I was taught to say my prayers by the woman that raised me and I have asked God in earnest what I should do about this crime and, after much thought, it has come to me that I am still a young man and can do much good in the world and so it is best that I live.

23

My only regret is that I did not kill more of them. The job was left undone. But I have sons and I am certain that they will continue the war as soon as they are old enough to fight. I give this message to my sons: Take up the rifle and the knife and kill the white men and keep killing them until they are no more.

I came late to the Agency and saw nothing but corpses among the burnt buildings. Where the Indians had taken flour, white trails lead over the meadows and among the trees in the woods and, when I saw those marks on the ground, I felt ashamed. With some boys, I went down to the ferry and met the soldiers who were trying to come across the river. We shot them mid-stream and they swallowed water and, later, I saw the big snapping turtles feasting on their bodies. Then, we went into the country to the cabins. We shot the men first so that they could not harm us as we molested their women and children. We cut off the teats of the women that we raped and, then, when we were finished with them, put torches flaming with pine-pitch between their legs and up into their wombs. We took their little children and cut them into small pieces so that you could put their parts into a bucket for water or slops. We sliced open pregnant women and took out their babies and nailed them to the doors of their shacks. We hacked off hands and feet and wore them dangling around our necks. We broke infants on stumps the way you smash open a pumpkin or a watermelon. It was as if we had drunk deeply of the white man's rum and his whiskey. We went about the countryside as if we were intoxicated, like wild men, and the land blossomed with smoke and fire behind us.

For three days, we hunted white people. After the first day of killing, the farmers fled and we had to take them from swamps and marshes where they crouched in the mud and dirty water. We pulled them out of trees that they had climbed and took them from the thickets where the thorns snarled their hair and ripped their trousers. We set the tall grass on fire where we knew that they were hiding and laughed to hear their screams as the flames burned them. We went farther abroad where our killings were only rumors and dragged the Dutchmen and the Swedes from their log cabins up in the Big Woods and cut them to pieces. On the last day, the prairie was empty and the woods were still and the only sound around their shanties was the snuffling of pigs feeding on the corpses. We rode all day from place to place but saw only dead people, most of them stripped naked and all tattooed with the marks that the ravens and crows made in their flesh. Finally, we found a small boy who was carrying his baby brother on his back. He was shoeless and his skin was all cut to tatters by the brambles and, when we gutted his baby brother, he took a pointed stick and charged at me and we spent several minutes batting him away from our ankles and knees. Then, I took him on my horse, because he had shown courage, and we went back to the camp, the boy crying the whole way.

My aunt has taken the white boy away with her to the Black Hills. Perhaps, he will fight with us also when he grows older. I told the women that he should be raised as a real human being because he showed heart and that we had rescued him from the whites who are not real men. All my sons will avenge me. I am sure of that. Outside I hear the guards singing about the baby boy born in the hay barn. This cold night is big medicine to the whites. Tomorrow or next day, they will hang me. I only wish I had killed more of them.

24

My brother's cousin was a little boy, but very fierce. He was like a small dog that is always hurling itself into the jaws of bears and wolves. He shook me awake in the hour when birds greet the sun and, when we saw the men leaving the village for the fight at the soldier's house, we slipped from our tipis and followed them.

The woods were dark and cluttered with deadfall and the men went swiftly without speaking, single-file, each leading his horse. The sky was light but it was still gloomy twilight beneath the trees and, when we stumbled over some fallen timber, the men turned around and shooed us away. We said that we would hold their horses during the fight. The leader told us that there would be many guns at the soldier's house and that we would be a burden upon the warriors and, then, without any more words, he departed and the troop with him and we were left alone to puzzle out why the men had been so silent and looked so grim with their foreheads all wrinkled with worry and their way of walking so quiet and light upon the earth.

Then, we found the other boys who had come from the village and crossed the river in the shallow place where the dead soldiers were bobbing about in the backwaters between the roots of trees and tangles of drifting brush. My brother's cousin wanted to cut the soldiers into pieces but we said that they were dirty, nasty things. Then, we went up on the prairie and saw the missionaries in their black frocks coming clumsily between the sloughs along the federal road. We lay in wait to ambush them, crouched down by the muddy water where the black flies buzzed and the mosquitos made clouds around us. My brother's cousin said to crawl on our bellies between the little oozing springs close enough to charge the missionaries and the cut-hairs with them. He went a little ways wiggling like a snake in the reeds and, then, suddenly a big, fat skunk appeared, lumbering forward like a badger and completely unafraid to come into our midst. We scattered to avoid the skunk, rolling on our sides this way and that, and, then, someone said that the ambush was spoiled. There was a quarrel about whether to attack, but the skunk had spoiled the ambush. My brother's cousin said that we would have beat out their brains one and all if the skunk had not driven us away.

Later, we met a Dutchman coming along the lane that lead to the federal road. He had a gun with a glittering barrel. We were afraid of his gun and backed away from him when he waved it at us. Then, my brother's cousin made his war cry and jumped at the Dutchman. The gun bounced as it was fired and there was a ring of blue smoke that punched through the air and, then, my brother's cousin was sitting on the ground with both hands holding his guts tight against his belly. The Dutchman tried to reload but we clubbed him to death and killed the others also. I showed my brother's cousin the gun that we had taken and he said that it was a very fine trophy and, then, he turned his face to the grass and died.

The women in the village held me responsible for the death of my brother's cousin because he was smaller and younger. They cried and demanded that we show them where we had hidden his body. The woods and trails looked different after the fighting and we could not find the place and, then, it was a relief when the soldiers came and took us away. Better to be hanged than to face a woman's scolding tongue.

25

It is not a pleasant thing to eat my porridge and boiled beef lying on my belly with the fetters gouging my shins. A wound in the buttocks is a funny thing so long as it is not on your own body. You can see how I have been hurt, and how the wound has festered. I would not have you think that I took this hurt fleeing from battle like a boy or a woman -- rather, you should know that I was downed in the cross-fire while fighting bravely.

I was wounded the second time we attacked the Dutchmen's town. At dawn on that day, we lit a big fire on the bluffs overlooking the village. This fire made the white men believe that the soldier's house, which lay farther east atop those hills, was again under attack and in need of help. We saw a group of horsemen leave the town and go in the direction of the smoke. There were less guns in the village and so it was time to make our charge on that place.

It was our grandest day, all the war chiefs on their prancing ponies and the soldier's lodges in full feather and fringed cape and with a thousand guns we rushed upon the town. Then, the grass was all on fire under our moccasins and the white men came out of their holes like prairie dogs frightened by the blazing grass and ran away from us. We swarmed among their buildings and put them to the torch and, then, suddenly found that there was rifle-fire coming from all directions and knocking us down. The smoke was very heavy and, after a while, creeping along the ground, we could not see one another and did not know whether the attack was continuing ahead of us or to the sides or whether we should fall back to clear the white snipers from the brick houses and the big wooden windmill.

For many hours, we fought in small groups, scrambling behind little stick-fences or hiding in shanties to shoot at the houses or the piles of barrels from which the white men were firing. Sometimes, we drove the white men from their defences and killed them as they ran, but other times, they would not move and so we circled, looking for other targets. The chiefs tried to gather us together and make us fight in one location, but that was a mistake -- every time, we formed a group in one place or another a party of white men would run howling at us, waving their guns and shooting and so we were broken again into many small groups, hiding behind wrecked wagons and burning walls.

In the late afternoon, we all lay close to the ground and shot in the direction of the enemy but were too thirsty and tired to attack. Then, a white man on a great charging horse leaped over the burning barricade and came against us. The white man was very brave and his horse was magnificent and we shot him down in the middle of the ruts and mud between two houses. Then, I went forward, singing my death song, to count coup on him because this white soldier had shown great courage and it would be an honorable thing to take his scalp. I struck his body with my stick but was shot in the buttocks by one of our own men firing blindly into the smoke.

The wound festered and, when I tried to flee a few weeks later, I was too sore to ride. I tried to mount my horse but the wound hurt me too terribly and, for this reason, I could not escape and so will be hanged.

26

Kill them all. Let no enemy escape. This is the rule of war. Because I violated this rule, I am waiting to be hanged.

On the day before the first fight at the Soldier's House, I lead a war-party across the river to set an ambush along the Federal Road. We caught some Dutchmen escaping from their town, driving wagons heavily laden with bedsteads and blankets and many other fine wares. Two boys walked in advance of the company, fearfully waving their guns at the tall grass. We charged at them and the boys dropped their guns and ran away. One of the Dutchmen on the wagons fired his gun at us. We shot him down before he was able to fire again. The other Dutchmen leaped down into the middle of the road. They all knelt together and raised their hands to protect their faces. We began to kill the men first by clubbing them with the guns that the boys had dropped in the middle of the road. One of the women stabbed at us with a butchering knife and fought bravely, lunging and slashing until I shot her in the belly. Even then, she tried to cut at our ankles and legs and obliged us to use another bullet to stop her from doing us any more mischief. Then, we were able to conserve rounds of ammunition by beating the rest of them to death. It was heavy work and we were sweating a good deal and, when I looked up from clubbing some of the children, I saw the two boys that had run away standing on the edge of a ravine, gawking at us and crying, but afraid to approach. One of my men asked if we should pursue them down the ravine but I was tired with smashing out of the brains of the Dutchmen and their women and little ones and so I said that we had done enough harm for one day and didn't need to hasten to kill the boys. "Someone else will get them," I said. We spared the oxen so that they could draw the wagons to our village and distributed our loot among all of the tipis.

During the second day of fighting at the fort, I lead an assault on the wagon gun at the corner of their defenses that was doing so much harm to us. The cannon jammed and could not be fired for several minutes and the soldiers behind the barricades were young and very nervous so that they fired their rifles either below us, kicking up fistfuls of sod, or, harmlessly, over our heads. I came so close to the wagon gun that I could see the fat, bearded soldier laboring over the muzzle: he was black as a bear with burnt gunpowder and glistening with sweat. The bearded man's eyes were white with fear and I saw him crank down the wagon gun and, then, there was a burst of fire. I fell to the ground and, when I looked behind me, no one was there. Some of our men lay on the grass ripped into two and three pieces the way you would tear a worm apart and others were crawling about blindly, as if searching for their eyes that had been shot out of their heads. I was too close to the fort to retreat and so I crept up to the breastworks and surrendered to one of the soldiers. Then the white men beat me with the muzzles of their guns until I was unconscious.

In the next few weeks, I helped the white soldiers. I scouted for them and showed the troops hidden paths and trails. The white men gave me a hat and blue coat and said that I was a good friend to them. But, one day in the autumn, after most of the leaves had fallen, two white boys came out of the thickets more dead than alive and accused me of killing Dutchmen on the Federal Road. Although I denied what they said, the white men did not regard me as such a friend that they would believe what I said against others of their own kind. And so I will be hanged tomorrow.

27

Before the fight at the Dutchmen's town, I promised my grandmother that I would burn the buildings and the distilleries until no trace of them remained. My grandmother said that this would be a good thing and that she would pray for my success. You see, the Dutchmen poisoned my uncle. They traded whiskey and rum to him for robes of buffalo fur and beaver pelts and fine tanned leather. He abandoned his family and, because there were no other sons, left his grandmother to starve. In the end, when he had nothing else to trade, he sold himself to the white men and did their errands so that they would let him wallow outside their taverns and saloons. They beat him like a dog and, in the cold season, his fingers and toes were so badly frozen that they fell off his body and, at last, when he could no longer haul water and firewood for them, they sent him back to us. His skin was green then and his insides were rotted away and, after vomiting blood for several days, he died. Then, my grandmother said that it would be better for us all to die in battle then to perish like her son. But no one did anything until the boys came back from the Big Woods with blood on their hands and we knew the white soldiers would be coming for them and so we had no choice but to try to kill all the settlers who had taken our land.

We charged across the prairie, spreading out to encircle the town, and, then, the white men retreated, drawing us into ambushes in the smoky alleyways and streets. The fighting was confusing and, often, the smoke was so dense that I could not see the river or the bluffs and, sometimes, did not know if the shadows that I was shooting at were our soldiers or white men. Everything was on fire: the dung heaps and garbage piles were burning and barrels rimmed with flame rolled along the street and their houses were on fire and the churches also, with the bells ringing in the towers.

In the afternoon, I came out of a ravine from which I had been shooting and crossed a pasture to where a big brick smokestack pointed up and away from some sheds all crawling with orange flames. Barrels were lying in the ruins and some of our men were kneeling to drink from where the bullets had broken the wood. The men said that the whiskey in the barrels gave them courage. They told me to drink. Bees and wasps were swarming all about. I said no and, then, several of the boys crawling between the barrels all gushing whiskey yellow as honey, clutched at themselves and fell forward and we saw white men coming up the hill, a dozen of them, all firing their guns and yelling and, at the head of their party, a white man on a fine, swift horse. We were outnumbered and fell back into the ravine where we could hide behind the deadfall. Several of our boys lay wounded among the barrels and the white men shot them each in the face and, then, began drinking the whiskey themselves. Someone found a ladle and handed it to the man on the horse and he filled his belly with whiskey. Then, they fired a few shots in our direction and hurried back down the hill so that they vanished into the smoke.

We went back to the broken barrels and drank some more. Then, I charged about the battle, helter skelter, darting in and out of the smoke, and I was no longer afraid because I knew that the bullets could not hurt me. We came back to the burnt distillery several times and, when I woke up the next morning, alone in the tall grass, I thought that we had won the battle because the town was all burnt to ashes. I stood up and two little white boys captured me. They lead me on a tether as if I were a pet raccoon or motherless bear cub.

28

This fellow fettered by my side is a loud-mouthed good-for-nothing and he makes our hours of confinement tedious with his prattle of Jesus and green meadows and heavenly herds of buffalo without number. He is acting shamefully and, I am certain, will disgrace himself on the scaffold. My missionary comrade, who speaks so much now about the Blood of the Lamb, was among the worst of the murderers during the war with the whites. He is one of Cut Nose's people and took many scalps when we were killing the white settlers: he cut the hair both from the heads of the man and from the crotches of the women that he raped before hacking them apart and. although I did similar things, I have not repudiated my actions and bent my head before the Black Robes and begged to them that they bestow their medicine upon me.

So you ask: why do I nod when this missionary Indian preachs to me? Why do I cock my head to hear him and pretend to agree with his words? Why have I been so amiable and friendly in the face of this nonsense that he spews from his mouth without ceasing day or night?

Here's is my plan: on the morning that we are to be hanged, the Black Robes will free this preacher of theirs to help them distribute the fry-bread that they believe to be the body of their Christ. My talkative friend has said this to me and he has asked if I will help him with this task and go among the fettered and chained men with the bread and bring each of the condemned this morsel. So I will be unchained as well and free to move about the prison house and I have heard that there is a man on the other side of the prison, whose eye the white women knocked out on our march, and who hides in his blankets a knife made of good steel.

With the knife, I will kill as many guards as possible and slash the Black Robes as well and, I suppose, the white soldiers will stab me to death with the knives that they fasten to the muzzle of their guns or, even, be obliged to shoot me down. In this way, I will die fighting and not without first sustaining many honorable wounds. I am not afraid to be run-through by their knives which are like the lances that we make and that the Crows have brought against us, nor am I frightened of bullets shot from their guns. A man can die only once and it is better by far to be killed with weapons wielded by other brave men than to die strangling at the end of a noose.

29

Sometimes, I wonder if all this misery arose from a misunderstanding. I don't think this is the case because there were many reasons that we went to war and no single cause is sufficient, in itself, to explain everything. But now that I am to be hanged for my part in this fighting, I wonder sometimes whether it was not a misunderstanding, or, worse, intentional deceit that has brought us to this state of affairs.

When the annuities did not arrive from the Great Father, we were very hungry. The buffalo herds had withdrawn to the west, beyond the bad lands of the White River, and, in order to reach them and take meat, it was necessary that the men in the hunting party have good guns and ammunition, that their ponies be fat and well-fed, and that they have sufficient boiled beef and flour to make the long hungry trip. But none of this could be accomplished without money from the annuity payments and so the hunters remained in our villages, frustrated and impatient for the arrival of the money.

But the money did not come and, after a few weeks, the trader said that he could not keep providing eggs and flour and beans on credit. The trader told us that he was a great friend to the Lakotah but also only the servant of another man and that the other man did not want the Indians to grow fat on credit. Someone then brought forth his little daughter who was sick with the flux and dying and another man brought his wife whose breasts were so fallen and empty that she could not nurse her baby and others came as well and stripped off their blankets to show their shrunken bellies all outlined in rib bones and said: Does this look like we are growing fat? Then, the trader apologized and invited us into his store to drink some coffee with him and smoke one of his cigars.

We talked with the trader a good deal in the store and someone said, as I remember, it is too bad that people can't eat the buffalo-grass because it is so abundant and could feed a nation of men as it has fed the hooved nations. I don't recall who made that statement, but we all agreed that it was a shame that the world was as it was and that human beings needed flour and beans and meat in order to live. The trader's wife, then, came and put some porridge meal and hardtack on the porch for us. But the meal was all crawling with worms and sticky with their leavings and the hardtack was dry as dust and impossible to swallow.

That night, the boys came down from the Big Woods and told us that they had killed several white people when stealing eggs for their breakfast. At first, the war chiefs all said that we should turn the boys over to the soldiers at the Fort because surely no one would grant us credit for food unless we cooperated with the authorities. Then, a man who had been in the trader's house said that the Indian Agent had spoken these words: If the Lakotah are hungry, let them eat grass. That was different from what I remembered but I didn't say anything. The man repeated those words -- they should eat grass like buffalo -- and there was great anger, then, among the leading men. I felt that I should say something since I remembered the Trader's words differently, but the young men were already making their war dance and painting their faces and the old men were still and grave as death itself, issuing orders through lips stretched tight as bow-strings, and so I was afraid and kept silent.

30

On the first day of the fighting, I did not kill any white people. I thought of them as our neighbors. I had traded with them and done small errands on their farms. I am ashamed to say that I drank their beer and spirits. The white people near our village I knew by their names and they called me "Johnny," although that is not what I am called in our language. Don't mistake me for a Cut-Hair. I was simply curious about the way that they lived.

On the second day, I went with the raiders. For three more days, I joined in the attacks. We killed them in their cabins and fields. We caught them in lonely places where they had gone to hide, always leaving trails as broad as a wounded bear, and killed them there also. We killed them on the road as they tried to flee. Some of the people knew my name and, when we came to kill them and their children, they cried out and asked me for mercy. As we bludgeoned them, they tried to take my hand or clutched at my garments. A woman handed me her baby and said that I should keep it safe since she knew that she had to die. I didn't kill the baby but left it on the prairie for the wolves. We pushed another woman into a fire that we had lit in her cabin. I had known her for many years. The woman cried out to me: "Johnny, Johnny, don't do this to me." Then, she kept jumping out of the fire, or, after her feet were burned off, rolling away from the flames and so I had to push her back into the burning cabin several times and, at last, burnt my own fingers and wrenched my back.

Then, I went to my tipi and was sick for many days. My back hurt me so badly that I could not walk and I lay on my buffalo pelts groaning and writhing with pain. I couldn't sleep at night and the dark hours were agony to me. Where I had burnt my fingers, the wounds festered and my fingernails turned black and fell off. I thought of the dead white people and wished that I could die also.

But I didn't die and, gradually, I was sick only at night, when the bad dreams kept me from sleeping. Then, the war chief came and said that every man was needed to drive the soldiers from our land. He told me that I could not be sick any longer and that it was time to fight against the blue-coats and all of us had to go, even the very old and the boys and the sick. So I went with the war party to the little lake near the Yellow Medicine Agency and, before dawn, we gathered together behind a ridge, men from all of the villages and clans along the river, many hundreds of us. The plan was that a party would attack the soldier's camp from the opposite side and draw fire and, when the wagon guns were aimed away from our direction, we would rise up and charge over the ridge and overwhelm them. But we heard shooting before we were marshalled for the attack and, then, the boom of the wagon-guns sounded and the war chiefs said that the plan had gone wrong. I was relieved because I didn't know if I had the stomach to fight. We put aside our weapons and hid our rifles and went back to our villages to await the soldiers.

That morning, the soldiers had found potatos growing in the gardens deserted at the agency. Some of their men had left the camp early and without orders to dig the potatos so that they could eat them for breakfast. The soldiers were tired of eating dried beef and biscuit-bread. It was those soldiers going to steal potatos that happened upon our war party just as the sun was rising and ruined our plans. I learned this later in the prison where I am waiting to be hanged.

31

After the older men went to fight at the Soldier's House, I gathered a party of boys from our village and lead them across the river. We saw the cut-hairs driving the wagons of the missionaries between the wet lands. I said that it was foolish to waste time killing these white people because they had never harmed us and, further, could be slaughtered at any time since they chose to live unarmed among us. A wild young boy, the cousin of one of my cousins, urged that we attack them and, went ahead with some of his friends, to lay an ambush in the tall grass. After a few moments, the boy came back, trembling like a leaf and saying that a skunk had come across his way and forced them to retreat to the main party. I said to the boy that he was a woman to be afraid of a skunk. Then, he called for us to advance again and assault the missionaries. Just at that moment, someone saw a flash as if from the muzzle of a gun among the missionaries. They had encamped for a moment between two marshes. We waited for the gun's report but no sound came. Some said that the missionaries were traveling with soldiers as well and that we had just seen them fire one of their new guns.

We rode away from the missionaries and looked for cabins built by the white men where the ravines dropping to the river slit open the prairie. The houses were all burnt and the people lying dead in the ashes or sprawled in the fields where the cattle were trampling the corn and crying out. Some of the younger boys shot arrows into the corpses but I told them that this was a cowardly thing to do.

We met a Dutchman traveling with his women. He stood up on the buckboard of his wagon and tried to parley with us. One of the older women lifted a blanket and removed a bird-gun that was hidden beside her which she handed to the Dutchman. The little girls were crying and hugging one another and putting their hands up to cover their eyes. The Dutchman held the gun as if it were a snake or some other repulsive animal. He kept the gun away from his body and tried to make his lips smile at us. The wild boy and his cousin said to me that they would kill one of the girls in front of the Dutchman and that, even then, he would be afraid to fire the gun at us. I said that the boy should first take the gun away from the Dutchman. The boy said he would kill both little girls first by beating out their brains with his club. I said to the boy that he should get the gun first for a trophy. "The Dutchman will give it to you and, then, you can shoot him in the face with his own weapon," I said. The boy hesitated and so I said: "Is this another skunk?" The boy cried out in anger and, running up to the Dutchman, reached to take the gun from him. The Dutchman shot the boy in the belly. Then, we pierced him with arrows but let him live long enough to see his women dead on the grounds with their heads smashed open like ripe gourds. The boy died and we hid his body.

It is unfair that I should hang for this. There are many who did far worse acts, but they have fled to be with our relatives on the buffalo-grass prairies beyond the river that the white men call the Missouri. My mother is not well and so I stayed in the village to assist her and make certain that she had enough meat and berries for the winter and, because I did not run away like the others, I was taken by the soldiers, condemned because of the Dutchman's gun which the white men had found, and, now, must hang.

32

Those who call me a killer are liars. I hurt no one in the recent unpleasantness with the white men. I am so sure of my innocence that I have told my mother and sisters that I will be with them the day after the hanging. Both the Black Robes and the guards say that the number condemned to be hanged is 38. Yet, there are 39 men confined in this prison house. One of us will be pardoned -- that is what they have told us -- and allowed to go free just before the others are executed and I am that man.

That first night, when the young men burst into camp on horses half ridden to death, they said that they had killed some white settlers, including women, in the Big Woods. They said "we have started this war with the shots that we have fired and there will be fighting whether you want it or not." Then, the war-chiefs met in counsel and I was there for my family is numerous and Cut Nose is my uncle and I said we should not harm any more white people and that the boys who had murdered the settlers in the Big Woods were fools who should be tied hand and foot and surrendered to the soldiers. But the others mocked me so I withdrew to my tipi and remained there for several days. I was not with the war parties that went to kill the traders and burn the agency and I did not participate in any raids against the white farmers. I have a gift for medicine and, when some of our men were hurt, I ministered to them with roots and herbs and bound up their wounds and, in gratitude, they gave me the watches and women's jewelry and the linens from the cabins found in my tipi when I surrendered. These watches and fabric mean nothing. Those who testified that I was among the killers are liars. They lie about me from envy because I am the nephew of Cut Nose who is known to be a very great man among our people.

A boy told me that there was a white woman in distress and that I should look to her and bring my medicines and so I left camp on the first day of fighting at the Soldier's House. The boy misled me and I found myself among those attacking the fort but my gun malfunctioned and I was not able to fire it. The next day, I hurried to the Dutchmen's town for the purpose of warning the people there that our war parties were coming, but I lost my way in the sloughs and arrived only after the attack was underway. I watched the battle but did not take part. I tried to warn the soldiers at the fort of our second attack as well, but had trouble crossing the river since the thunderstorm on the preceding day had dangerously swollen the stream. At last, I forded the river, but too far downstream to reach the Soldier's House before the attack began. I did not even have a firearm in my possession on that day.

By this time, my wife and children were hungry because the traders had all been killed and no game had been taken to feed the people. I spent the next day searching the river bottoms for water fowl and, so if anyone saw me with a rifle near the Dutchman's town, that was because game trails lead me close to that fighting. Some white men shot at me, but I did not return their fire. I was with the party of men who ambushed the burial party near the coulee, but that was because someone had told me that we were going to flee west, beyond the Black Hills, and I was riding with those men when the attack happened. Another warrior's gun misfired and he took my weapon and shot at the soldiers although I tried to make him miss by pushing against his shoulder. I was called to the fight at Wood Lake but only to care for our wounded and I didn't carry a weapon that day. I saw some others fire at the soldiers a little later in the afternoon but they were at a great distance and I'm pretty sure no one was hit.

Everyone understood what the distances meant: the soldiers in the fort could not hurt us without coming from behind their barricades and advancing, at least, to the shelter of the barrel-shaped brick house where they kept ice hacked from the river and where, in fact, several sharpshooters were stationed. Bullets fired from the fort itself could not carry to the ravine where we crouched among the trees, now and then, shooting back in their direction although we knew that our shots were equally ineffective. A few bullets aimed into the sky fell among us, hot to the touch, but, otherwise, too weak to harm anyone. There was no real danger on either side although both firing lines, ours and the men in the soldier's house, made a great deal of racket.

For the most part, it was a pleasant afternoon, cool in the shade and with a little stream of water laughing in our ears when the volleys of musket fire fell silent. Women came from the villages and roasted beef and corn in the glen below the top of the ravine where we hid among the tangled brush and deadfall aiming our guns at the Fort.

When I was young, I went on raids and took many horses. I followed the buffalo west to the Black Hills and the Bear Lodge. A Crow Indian once cut me in the thigh with his lance before I knocked him from his mount and took his scalp. I've been frozen in blizzards that burst suddenly from clouds no bigger than my fist and burnt by the sun until the carrion birds thought I was too dry and roasted to be worth pecking at. I've been a dreamer and a prophet and had my flesh ripped in the Sun Dance and, now, that I'm an old man, I would like nothing better than to sleep away what remains of my life. This prison, where we are fed twice daily, is as good a place as my tipi to drowse away the rest of my days and, although I am being hanged for crimes I didn't commit, there were plenty of other offences for which I am guilty that were never alleged against me.

And it isn't defeat in battle that has made me so careless about what remains of my life. I felt this way at the fight at the Soldier's House. My belly was full and it was good to nap even with the guns crashing around me and, when the war-chief came to tap me on the buttocks with his coup-stick, and push me forward, I said that my legs were too stiff to go running into that rifle-fire but that I might crawl a few feet toward the fort so that my shots would be within range. Many of the boys went whooping toward the fort, dashing and jumping and criss-crossing to avoid the bullets, but the rotten shot knocked them down like men at a pow-wow drum smashed by lightning. Then, a solid shell came from the fort, hopping like a toad toward us, and the war chief put out his foot to kick at the cannon-ball and show us that it was spent and could not hurt anyone. The cannon-ball tore off the chief's leg, ripping his foot and calf away from his raw, white knee-cap, and, then, bouncing, the shell knocked out the brains of another boy kneeling nearby. The men scrambled to find a rope or twine to tie off the blood spurting from the knee-bones but it was too late: the war chief sat down among the leaves, sighed several times, and, as his lips moved to make his death song, the light left his eyes and he died.

We gathered the meat and roast corn that the women had cooked in the ravine and went back to our village. Some of the younger men hid the war-chief's body so that the white men would not know that they killed him. I kept to my tipi after that and fought no more.

34

Afraid of hanging? Bah! No one will hang me. My escape plan is fool-proof. I look forward to the day that the great gallows, big as a house built of sticks, is complete. That will be the eve of my freedom from this dark and sti-fling place. Look for me, then, beyond the Missouri and north across the border in Grandmother's Country where the soldiers from this land can not pursue.

Brave words, you might say, from a one-eyed man. When we were dragged in chains through the village by the river, a white woman came and scooped out this eye of mine. The she-devils beat us with sticks and stabbed our blankets with kitchen knives and, if the white soldiers, had not leveled the blades on their gun-muzzles at that mob none of us would have survived. So I am left with a scab for an eye, but, in that frenzy, one of their bitches dropped her butch-er knife and, even, half-blinded, I saw the steel edge lying in the frozen mud and stooped and put it between my belt and my belly and, for this reason, I am armed today, although there are only a few to whom I have told this.

On the dawn that we are to be hanged, the Black Robes have promised to come among us with that flat-bread that they call the Body of their God and they will bow their heads in prayer and an Indian, pretending to believe as they be-lieve, will assist in the distribution of that bread. When he comes to me, I will wink with my one eye that is still alive and he will wink as well, and as he passes me the Body of their God, I will slip the knife into his hands. The Black Robes will close their eyes to mutter another prayer and, when they are helpless, the Indian will throw the wafer away and cut them down. Then, he will dash to the little guardhouse where the sentry is always sleeping and slit his throat and, in that shack, I have seen an axe and a mallet. With axe and mallet, we will break our chains and rise up to strangle the guards as they come into us through the narrow, barred door to drag us onto the parade-ground where the gallows has been built.

I have sent word of this rising far beyond this prison. When my wife vis-ited and cried about my ruined eye, I told her it was a small price to pay for our escape. She has sent messages west and I am told that all our relations our coming now to our rescue -- the Minneconju, the Brule and Oglala, the Teton and the Sans Arc, the Two Kettles people as well and many Cheyenne from the plains -- all our riding their ponies in this direction and they will encircle the town and make the skies black with the smoke of their council fires and, when the day comes to hang us, a great multitude of our warriors will come down from the river bluffs and burn the stick houses and tear down the brick walls and we will come from this prison to meet our brothers and their soldiers will die like buffalo calves in the cold moon when the wolves hunt them.

Remember what I have told you tomorrow, when the bell tolls, and the Black Robes with their grey faces come among us and you hear the death-songs from those who have not believed what I have said. Lay your head down on this iron-hard, frozen earth and listen attentively and, already, you will hear the hoof-beats of a thousand horses come thundering across the prairie to save us.

35

I did many things in the fighting and, although I did not kill as many white people as some, I cut down my share of them and so, I suppose, that there is no wrong done by hanging me. We would have killed them all if we could have and so they will now kill as many of us as their laws allow. Just let my women know that I was not afraid and have no regrets. Tell my children I died like a man.

In the fight at the fort, during the second day, Cut Nose disgraced my brother. A shell sailed overhead and my brother flinched when it burst and sprayed metal on us. Cut Nose said that my brother was squinting like a dog that has been beaten and that a man who squints in battle is one whose mother was entered from behind when he was being made. This would not have been so bad, but a young woman dear to my brother had come with us to roast corn and beef on spits in the ravine below the place where we were fighting and she was carrying water up the slope to the firing line when Cut Nose spoke in this way to my brother. My brother lunged at Cut Nose, but the older man was strong and swift and knocked him down. Cut Nose called my brother "Squint Eye" and told him to go to the women and help them make us something to eat. My brother's face was red and his eyes became wet and he ran away.

We joined the fight at the Dutchmen's town and my brother went in the forefront of the war party, always leading every advance to show that he was not afraid. We swallowed smoke in that battle and fought choking and, every time a group of us gathered to make an attack, the white men dashed through the haze and shot some of us down and, when we rallied to counter-attack, they were hidden behind their fences of barrels and smashed furniture.

Late in the afternoon, when we were too tired to sprint about the burning town, most of us found protected positions and poured as many bullets as we could into the shacks and fortifications where the white men were concealed. Then, suddenly, a man mounted on a very fine pale horse came charging through the smoke. The haze seemed to make him seem much larger than any other enemy that we had seen that day and he towered over the burnt-out cellars from which we were firing. Many guns shot at him and he was hit again and again, but still the horse pranced forward and was not afraid and, although the man was dying, he did not fall to the ground until he was almost among us. Then, my brother, who had been fighting at my side, said that he would count coup on this white soldier because it was a fine thing to strike a blow against so courageous an enemy. My brother cried out and ran forward, leaning forward as if he were walking against the wind of a cyclone, and, somehow, he reached the place where the horseman had fallen. He tapped the dead man with his coup-stick and, then, was shot down. I crawled on my belly to where my brother was lying. The white man lay dead a few feet away, blood draining from a dozen holes in his belly and chest, and he smelled very sweet and foul, like a field where a thousand apples have fallen from the trees and been left to rot. I rolled my brother away from the corpse, pushing him like a hunk of firewood, and, just before I reached safety, a bullet came from somewhere and broke my knee and so I could not escape to the Black Hills like many others have done.

My brother is not a coward. I have told this story to attest to his courage.

The whites are not men. They are devils. They are wolves slinking about the corpses of the dead. They are crows and ravens that pick out the eyes of wounded men left on the prairie. There is nothing human about them.

I protected several of their women in my tipi. Of course, I used them as would be customary with any woman captured in battle but I was not cruel and did not cut or mutilate them in any way. I sheltered those women from the other men, and when we had to strike camp and hurry away to the west, I did not kill them like many others killed their captives. Instead I fed them from my own fodder so that they ate as well as my own wives and children ate and, when we went hungry, all of us went hungry. After the fight at the swamp, we were promised amnesty if we surrendered and so I brought my captives to the soldier's camp and exchanged them for some blankets and dried corn. But when we tried to depart, the troops detained us and, after awhile, they built a stockade around our tents and, then, when it was cold and sleet fell from the skies and all the ways were wet and muddy if they weren't icy and frozen, we were chained together and marched across the open prairie.

The march was quick and many of the women were sick. Rain fell and sleet froze in our eyes and the soldier's used the knives on the ends of their guns to force us forward. Some of our children died and we were not allowed to dispose of their bodies until the end of the day's march so that the grieving mothers carried the dead little ones close to their breasts as they staggered forward and, I believe, that some of the women lost their minds in this way and asked to be shot and left for dead with their children.

Then, we were marched down a steep road and through a town built all along the river and there was only one path between the stick houses and the cold, icy water and, in the twilight, we could see a great black mob of women and boys gathered to block our way. The soldiers whispered among themselves and, after a long pause, prodded us forward. The white people surged all around us and would not open a path for us and, shrieking like demons, they hurled rocks and firewood and dead cats and other foul and filthy things down on our heads.. The air was full of projectiles and, when of our men chained to the others fell, we all slipped and plunged down onto the frozen ruts of the street and, then, the women and boys rushed upon us and kicked us with their boots and hit us with axe-handles and other clubs. We were spat upon and I saw two women seize a baby from a sick girl among us. The women smashed the baby against the wheel of a wagon and threw the broken infant onto a pile of offal. The soldiers growled at the mob and pointed the knives on their guns in their direction but they didn't fire and did nothing else to restrain the crowd of devils that were beating us to death.

Somehow, we came through the town and bleeding and battered marched several more miles before pitching camp in a bend of the river. The icy water rushed by us on three sides and I could hear the children coughing and the women crying and black ice fell on us from the sky. For all the world, I would not pass another night like that, without fire and under pitiless skies, with the women and children all crying out for help that we could not give to them. At least, when they hang me, I will be free of that memory which haunts me now like a terrible ghost.

Over the earth I come
Over the earth I come
Over the earth I come
Over the earth I come

The hawk is flying
The hawk is flying
The hawk is flying
Over the earth hawk flies.

The deer is running
The deer is running
The deer is running
Over the earth deer runs.

The wolf is howling
The wolf is howling
The wolf is howling
Over the earth wolf howls.

Death goes before me
Death goes beside me
Death goes above me
My hands smell of death.

Over the earth I come
Over the earth I come
Over the earth I come
Over the earth I come

38

We tried to turn back time. We thought that if we could kill enough white people, they would be frightened and run away from our country and that our world be restored to the way it was before they came among us. This was not a childish thing. We killed them in great numbers and in ways that were intended to create shock and awe at our cruelty and there was calculation involved as well -- we knew that the white men were slaughtering one another as herds of buffalo, when they stampede, plunge off cliffs and we thought that they would not be able to spare an army to punish us for what we had done.

War is our pasttime and sport and recreation. We are nothing without war and it was cruel of them to ban us from going on raids against the Chippewa and the Crow. But we do not make war like white people. White people make war as if it were a business and another way of buying and selling. They are willing to fight in the night-time when it is dark and those who fall in battle can not find their way to heaven because of the gloom. They fight in the rain that would ruin our feathers and regalia and turn our warriors into drab, drenched water-rats without any glory or beauty. They come against you in the snow and the ice when decent people are rest-ing in their tents and telling stories of old times. They kill you with steaming pieces of metal shot from a mile away so that death is not a matter of heroism or courage but a mere accident -- like being struck by one of their wagons on the Federal Road when staggering home drunk. Against this sort of people, we were powerless.

Tell my wife that she should seek out the Cut-Hairs among our people and have them teach my children to live among the white men. They should learn to read and write and reckon like the traders at the Agency. Perhaps, they should listen to what the Black Robes have to say since their God seems to have prevailed over our gods and it might be well to consider their religion as good medicine. It is probably best to learn the white men's ways so that we can live among them without further fighting. I am happy to die so that I will not have to change my ways.

I was raised at Kaposia where the sweet-water springs come clean and cold from the sandstone cliffs in the little gorge. We put our tipi-rings where the streams from the cliffs emerged from the canyon into the great river valley. We made hoops of willow and rolled them along the sandy shore of the river and the boys learned to shoot by trying to pass arrows through those hoops. Game was abundant and my mother's people lived across the big river and, in the winter-time, we walked across the ice and visited them in their village and there was much feasting. Once we re-pelled a war-party of Chippewa and chased them to the walls of the Soldier's House where the rivers join and killed them all under the gates of the Fort. We took our furs and bead-work to the trader's house made of brick and tall as a tree at Mendota and the white man gave us money so that we could buy guns and whiskey and bullets. When I was a boy, the white trader's wife, who was one of our people, gave me sugar candy that melted in the hollow of my cheek. In the Spring, we took water-fowl from the marshes around the river and, then, rode west to follow the buffalo and, once, we went as far as the Black Hills where I saw the windy hole in the rock from which the first buffalo had come and from which our people emerged. At the pip-estone quarries, I watched men carving fine pipes from the soft red stone that is the color of our skin. All these things are only memories now. And, soon, these memo-ries will be lost as well.

39

All night long, the older men talked of war. If nothing else, war makes memories. The older men remembered each wound they had ever taken or given. They spoke the names of warriors who had died in battle before I was born. The smoke from the council fire made their eyes red and moist. Those of us young enough to be capable of actually fighting in war had heard talk of this kind before. Nothing ever came of it: old men are full of talk.

Some of Cut nose's people kept the boys who had come down from the Big Woods with blood on their hands in a tipi set aside from the rest of the village. The men sitting outside that tent had rifles in their hands. Someone told me that Cut Nose was planning to turn the boys over to the soldiers the next morning and that his cousins were guarding them so that they would not escape and make more trouble. Cut Nose said that he was old and weary and that resting in his tipi had made him fat as a beaver and that he did not want to go on the war-path. After the boys had told us about the white people they killed, Cut Nose and the other head men had them taken from the council and confined in the tipi on the edge of the village. From this moment, Cut Nose said, this matter does not concern them. He was able to take them into his custody because several of the young men were his nephews.

I don't think anything was decided that night. I fell asleep and, several times, when I opened my eyes, I heard the voices of the older men droning on and on.

In the morning, I heard a popping sound. Some of the women told me that the boys had found a cache of firecrackers of the kind that the white men had shot off on their big flag holiday. That was only a few weeks before and the popping sound echoing through the sticky, hot morning air was the same. It as fun to play with the firecrackers and toss them on one another or at dogs or squirrels and so I left my brothers and sisters and hurried along the river-bluff paths to the Agency.

At the Agency, I saw that a house was burning and that the door to a storage building had been smashed apart. Men came out of the warehouse with their arms full of sacks of flour and beans. One fellow from our village was already drunk and he danced in circles in the dusty square between the houses, a long cape of cloth fluttering about his shoulders. The horses from the stables were loose and grazing in the meadow and, a few feet from where one of the ponies stood, I saw a white girl lying on her back with her dress pulled up to cover her face. She was not moving and blood had soaked through the part of the dress lying over her eyes. The dead girl's thighs were very pale so that the black hair thatching her groin looked very dark to me. I had never seen a naked white girl and so I squatted down to look between her legs. Then, I heard laughter and shouting. I stood up and saw a man coming from the trader's house. He was swinging something in his hands as if it were a bucket full of water from the pump. As he approached, I saw that he was carrying the trader's head by the hair and that the white man's mouth was all shaggy with grass that had been stuffed between his lips.

Then, I knew that I was seeing the war that we had talked about so much. I went to the village and all the older men were cleaning their rifles and the women were running bullets.

On Front Street

Before they lugged it off, the monument was plunked-down where the sidewalk widens in front of the Big Chief Bar. College kids kept stealing the stone and, once, some wild Indians from South Dakota dumped blood and guts all over the thing. They were trying to make some kind of point. But this sort of stuff is not good for business.

On the other side of Front Street, across from the Big Chief, there is another tavern, Bobbie's. Both of them are run by Bob the Barman, but he never comes to the neighborhood meetings because he works late hours managing the tow joints and sleeps during the day when decent folks are up and about.

Today, the boys from the neighborhood are plenty steamed. Ray, the barber, has just been served papers. The State of Minnesota wants the monument back behind the little chain fence, set between the stone benches that look as if they were carved by wind and water from identical slabs of granite.

-- Bob oughta be here, says Elmer, the Realtor. -- He's gotta dog in this fight just like the rest of us.

-- Bob's a great guy, don't get me wrong, says Wm. Bruce. -- but in the liquor business you gotta keep your nose clean and your head down and observe a low profile and, you know, he cant be counted on for advocacy in this dispute

-- But bob oughta be here, Elmer repeats, -- It's square in front of his places.

Wm. Bruce owns the frame and picture store. His storefront window is full of pictures of soldiers and pheasants. He wears a bowtie that he ties himself and spends one full week each year in New York City, mostly seeing the new Broadway musicals.

Zorba says -- I consult my attorney. He says it's a nuisance. That's law. The history thing is a nuisance. So we can sue back.

Ray is the one with his tit in the ringer. He's hangdog with a slump-shouldered, mouth-breathing look of dejection.

-- I just don't know, Ray says. -- I suppose we better put it back out there.

-- And bust up my back again, Zorba says. He gropes for a wounded spot on his spine. -- How can I work if my back is all bust-up?

-- Work? Elmer says under his breath.

Zorba is a bookie and he runs the card parlor kitty-corner to where the monument usually sits. He's from Lebanon where they sweat differently from here and his real name is something Arab, but, given these troubled times, and since his buddies have only a very approximate notion of middle-eastern phy, its best to let them think he's Greek -- hence the nickname.

geography, its best to let them think he's Greek – hence the nickname.

Zorba grins. – I work as hard as the next guy around here, he says.

It's mid-afternoon and they are sprawled in the barber's chairs and stiff-backed waiting benches in Ray's Barbershop. The sunlight is warm and suffusing cologne and hair pomade into the air. Water is dripping from a spigot. The monument is shoved up against a back wall, strapped to an industrial-sized dolly. It's a tombstone-shaped ashlar, polished smooth on the front face so that an inscription could be cut into the stone. The stone stands as tall as a ten-year old kid and is just as dumb and gawky. Broad, wrist-thick orange straps made from abraded canvas have been cinched tight around the stone's breast and belly. The straps cover the letters cut into the stone so that it reads:

On this site 38
Warriors of the
Santee Siou

303 men were convicted
Of rapes and murders committed
In the Sioux Uprising that had
Occurred earlier that year. President
Abraham Lincoln pardon

    ly 38
     actually hanged
   r their crimes. The event was the
largest mass execution in American
      History.

This monument placed by the County of blue
Earth and the State of Minnesota Historical
Societies – MCMVIII

Someone has tossed a panama hat over the pointy obelisk-top to the monument so that it seems to be giving the men a jaunty nod.

-- So what do we do? Ray asks. – Just put the son-of-a-buck back on the street?

-- Then what? Elmer says. – the Gusties will just sneak down here as homecoming and snatch the goddamn thing and, last time, that happened they drove all over the sidewalk and broke down the curbs and, you remember, Zorba…?

Zorba says: -- Pissed beer all over everything and somehow knocked out one of my windows.

Wm. Bruce shrugs: -- Then, the cops find the thing sitting out in the country somewhere and the State hauls the bastard back here.

-- And it just starts all over again, Elmer says.

www.ingramcontent.com/pod-product-compliance
Lightning Source LLC
Chambersburg PA
CBHW072231190626
46809CB00017B/1814